THE LAW REVIEW

S. Scott Gaille

CREATIVE ARTS BOOK COMPANY
Berkeley • California

For information contact:
Creative Arts Book Company
833 Bancroft Way
Berkeley, California 94710
1-800-848-7789
Fax: 1-510-848-4844
www.creativeartsbooks.com

ISBN 0-88739-377-2
Library of Congress Catalog Number 2002103449

Printed in the United States of America

THE LAW REVIEW

THE LAW REVIEW

To Sharin

ONE

It was a dreary October afternoon in 1992, but I was exactly where I wanted to be. I was starting law school at the University of Chicago, listening to Dean Simpson's welcome address to my incoming first-year or "one L" class. He concluded by charging all of us to "never fail to strive for excellence, and always to do what is right and good." It all seemed straight-forward enough, and I truly believed that it would be easy to comply with Dean Simpson's directions. Little did I know.

"Gray, let's beat the crowd," said Lee Gibbs, an old friend in his second year of law school.

I joined him in the aisle, where we struggled through the massive exodus of dazed one L's and out into the sterile white marble foyer with its imposing portraits of dead professors.

"This way," said Lee. He pointed to a glass door leading outside.

Without thinking, I pushed against the door only to have it hold firm. My body felt numb for a second, shocked from the collision.

"You'll have to memorize these doors if you're going to survive the first week."

The orientation program had warned us about the doors, which were designed to randomly open in different directions, symbolizing the maze of the law and the work that each of us would do here.

"See, it's a pull door," said Lee, pulling it open and motioning for me to go through.

I walked outside, still in a daze, and looked up to see a strange man in a suit running in our direction. "Stop," he yelled, waving his arms. "Go back!"

We froze.

"FBI," he yelled, now waving identification. "Get back inside!"

Before we could comply, he was upon us, pushing us back toward the door. Only the rest of the crowd was now emerging from the building. We were surrounded by dozens of other students. The agent released us and moved to take control of the crowd. "FBI. Everyone back inside! We have a situation out here!" The students who had passed us now turned around and tried to push their way back to the door. Everyone was yelling, "Go back! Go back!" Yet those who were inside continued to try to get out through the door, unaware of the danger. Lee and I were caught between the two groups, crushed in the crowd and unable to move, except for a few quick steps in this or that direction as the crowd had its way. Just when I felt that I could no longer breathe, the growing chorus of "Go back! Go back!" finally reached those inside. The opposing crowd relented, and we poured through the doorway.

Once we were all inside, the FBI agent shouted, "Go to an interior room!"

We moved quickly and silently toward the auditorium. I tried to look back to find out what was happening but could only see a kaleidoscope of scared faces.

When Lee and I took our seats in the auditorium, Dean Simpson was still at the podium chatting with lingering students. The FBI agent ran down the auditorium stairs, his badge drawn. He took the podium and addressed the crowd. "This is the FBI. There is a dangerous situation outside. When the situation is resolved, you will be so informed." The dean and the agent then left together.

"Are you all right?" Lee asked.

"Just some bruises around my ribs," I said, rubbing my chest. "How about you?"

"I'm okay."

"Did you see anything?"

"Some flashing lights."

"I didn't even see those."

We asked everyone around us whether they had seen anything but learned no more. About fifteen minutes later, another agent walked to the podium and announced that we could leave.

Lee and I made our way back outside. It was still pandemonium. Dozens of law enforcement vehicles were flashing their lights, including a Chicago police van that was adorned with big red letters: "**BOMB SQUAD**". Two officers dressed in full body armor, holding large hooded helmets in their hands, were standing next to the van. But someone else caught Lee's attention.

"Look, it's Miles Vanderlyden, the editor-in-chief of the *Law Review.*" Lee pointed toward a tall, dark-haired figure in a raincoat who was surrounded by FBI agents. Next to him, a police wrecker was in the process of towing a beige Honda Accord. As we walked by, I heard Miles saying, "There's no need to take my car."

I noticed a gleeful smile on Lee's face, which, by the time we arrived at his car, had grown to laughter. As we drove off, Lee was giggling so hard he couldn't steer straight.

I understood why Lee was reveling in Miles's misfortune. Just two months ago, Miles had denied Lee admission to the prestigious legal journal, the *Law Review.* Lee should've been in this revered group but for a twist of fate. His grades were good enough, but one further hurdle stood between him and membership. New members' applications had to be postmarked by a particular date. Lee, however, had waited until the last day to mail his application. That was the day he was starting a summer job at a Washington, D.C. law firm. When Lee, envelope in hand, asked the firm's managing partner for directions to the nearest post office, the partner grabbed Lee's application and handed it to a passing mail clerk. To his credit, Lee did stop by later in the day to make sure that his envelope was gone. It had indeed been mailed. Only the date of the firm's postage meter was off, set one day ahead by a temporary mail room employee. Because Lee's envelope was postmarked one day late, the three-member executive board of the *Law Review* disqualified his application.

"I'm going to get you on the *Review,*" said Lee, regaining his composure.

"You need to get back there first."

"That too." He adjusted his baseball hat, which hid his unwashed, greasy blond hair. "Then I want to help you."

"Thanks," I said.

It was strange to see Lee's star fall. All through college at the University of Texas, I had walked in the shadow of Lee's uniform excellence. Unlike Lee, I was average in most respects. Brown hair. Brown eyes. I possessed such average physical features that people would invariably not remember seeing me at parties, or even worse, confuse me with others. I never once received any athletic award, and I couldn't afford a flashy sports car. The only talent I had was that I was smart, really smart. But my peers never cared. I had come to the University of Chicago because it was the intellectual capital of the world. I desperately wanted to be noticed, appreciated. Lee was to be my mentor in this regard, but his slouched figure told me what I already knew. I'd have to find someone else.

I looked away from Lee, toward the downtown towers perched along the lake, their lights casting ghostly illuminations into the swirling dark clouds above. Immersed in these strange new surroundings and jarred by the day's events, I couldn't help but doubt my dreams.

TWO

At the Navy Pier law school orientation party, we boarded a double-decker sightseeing boat, the *Fort Dearborn.*

"How about a beer?" I grabbed two from a passing waiter's tray.

"Thanks," said Lee.

We worked our way to the vantage point of the bow. While Lee stared blankly off into the Chicago lakefront, I surveyed my intense classmates. That's when I noticed *her*, a beacon of energy even in this impressive crowd. Short, straight black hair, not quite shoulder length. Pale skin. Thin. Cute, but not beautiful. About five-four. Incredible poise and confidence. I watched her for a few minutes before distracting Lee from his thoughts with a tap on the shoulder.

"Yes?"

"Do you see that thin brunette, the one in the white sweater?"

I pointed discreetly, with my arm at waist level.

"The one who just took a sip from her cocktail?" he asked.

"Yes."

"She's not your classmate. She's a third-year student, presumably here helping with orientation." Lee turned pale.

"Well, what's her name?"

"Aris Byrd."

"Why does that name sound familiar?" I asked, turning for another glance.

"She's on the executive board of the *Law Review.*"

I felt goose bumps race across my back at the prospect of finding a new mentor. "There's something about her."

"She's evil," said Lee.

"Oh, please."

I looked back toward Aris, now finding her more than cute.

"She's really beautiful," I said.

"She certainly has an intangible charisma about her," conceded Lee.

"Which editor is she?"

"Topics and comments, the number three position, and the holder of the key to my future."

"I'm going to try to meet her," I said, "if only to find out what the hell happened to Miles today."

"There's one other thing," said Lee. He leaned closer.

"Yes?"

He lowered his voice to a whisper. "Look, if you even so much as think about repeating what I'm about to tell you, I'm screwed. If Aris ever knew I mentioned this to anyone, she'd wreck my appeal."

I nodded.

"Last year we sat together on a plane to Washington, D.C. Conversation was good, and that night we met for drinks. We talked and drank and one thing led to another—"

I interrupted. "If you and she have some kind of relationship, I'll forget about her."

He shook his head. "There's nothing anymore. When I screwed up with the *Law Review* application, it was over. I'm not 'in,' so Ms. Byrd can't even bring herself to acknowledge my existence, much less the fact that—"

"I understand," I said.

As I stepped back, Lee grabbed my arm. "Be careful with this one. She's more obsessed, more driven than anyone you'll ever meet."

Despite Lee's warnings, I worked my way through the crowd until I was within two bodies of Aris. I pretended to be mesmerized by the buildings while eavesdropping on her conversation with one of my female classmates.

"You shouldn't be too obsessed with *Law Review*," Aris explained, in a voice that carried a hint of Southern roots.

"I know," said the one L. "The opportunities here are the same for everyone regardless of grades."

"Where did you get that idea?" quipped Aris.

"That's what the students on an orientation panel said earlier today."

"Okay, sure, but while everyone at Chicago will get a job offer from the law firm of their choosing, there's a definite hierarchy of opportunity here. If you want a Court of Appeals clerkship, the *Review* is a prerequisite. No *Law Review*, no clerkship."

"Oh," mulled the one L.

"Don't worry Beth, *Law Review* will either come or not. It's all about your grades. My advice is work hard and stay focused."

"Thanks for the advice," muttered the bewildered one L.

I glanced over my shoulder to see Aris moving toward me. She now stood to my immediate right, only a foot away. I thought I could smell spices, notes in her perfume.

Just then, the boat lurched, and Aris nearly fell against me, spilling her drink across my shirt.

"Excuse me," she said, offering no further apology for the altered state of my clothing.

"I suppose we're finally under way," I said. "Hello, I'm Grayson Bullock."

"Aris Byrd."

We shook hands.

"Another drink?" she asked, flagging a passing waiter.

"Sure."

She took my beer and replaced it with a glass of white wine from the waiter's tray. She took a glass for herself as well.

"So what did you think of the commotion today?" she asked.

"I was basically tackled by an FBI agent. There wasn't a whole lot of thinking to do."

"Point well taken," she said, smiling broadly.

"I was, however, surprised to see Miles Vanderlyden's car being towed by the FBI. Do you know anything about that?"

Aris quickly recovered from a brief moment of surprise. "You know Miles?"

"I know who he is—who doesn't—but we've never met."

"Of course, he couldn't make it to this evenings festivities."

"I don't suppose I could talk you into telling me what happened?" I shot Aris my best boyish grin and leaned closer so that my leg brushed against hers.

She nodded. "Miles's father is a judge on the U.S. Court of Appeals in Miami. A few months ago he upheld the death sentence of one Ramon Cardenas, a notorious narcotics trafficker from Bolivia responsible for kidnapping and murdering an American petroleum executive."

"Sounds like a nice guy."

"Well, Judge Vanderlyden received a little gift from Cardenas's boys today. It was a die-cast metal car, about the size of a shoe box, the same make, model, and color as Miles's car, with his license plate number painted on. There was just one disturbing addition: little plastic pieces of dynamite glued to its underside."

"Oh." I was afraid I was gaping.

"Wish you hadn't asked?"

I smiled and took a drink. It was clear that Aris was through talking about Miles and his misfortunes.

"Why did you choose Chicago?" she asked.

"Over Yale or the Texas schools?"

"That should be obvious."

"Chicago was second to Yale in the national rankings when I submitted my applications. But while Yale is the darling of the left, Chicago's the most respected law school among conservative thinkers."

"I take it you're a Republican," she said.

"That being true, I thought Chicago was the superior choice."

"You'll like it here. It's about being something great, a part of something great."

"What do you mean?"

"If you do well here, doors will open in Washington."

"As in judicial clerkships?"

"That's right," she said, grabbing another glass of wine from a passing waiter. "The Supreme Court will hire thirty-six clerks this year. The vast majority will come from Chicago, Yale, Harvard, and Stanford—in roughly equal portions."

"Most of my friends back in Texas wouldn't understand. They're marching onward toward a big house and matching BMW's. It just wasn't for me."

"There are plenty of people aspiring to that here. Not everyone can be a Supreme Court clerk, and private practice isn't such a bad life."

"I want to contribute something more, though."

Aris took hold of my forearm and leaned closer. "If luck stays on my side, six months from now, I'll be holding an offer to clerk for the Supreme Court."

"After that, then what?"

"Perhaps the Department of Justice."

"You don't want to practice at a firm, even for a few years?" I asked.

"I want to be in the seat of power. How about you? Where do you ultimately see yourself?"

"Sometimes I hear this voice that says," I deepened my voice to mimic a master of ceremonies, "'And now, introducing the newly-elected junior senator from Texas.'"

"You do have a certain all-American charm—"

The music started playing, drowning Aris's voice. She leaned over and yelled into my ear, "Let's dance." I nodded.

As Aris led me by the hand to the dance floor, I felt a connection with her. We had both come to Chicago in pursuit of similar dreams, and I thought that Aris would be an excellent ally and guide through the treacherous first year of law school.

Once on the dance floor, Aris's physical grace cemented my attraction. She spun and connected effortlessly to the beat of the music, gliding in circles around me. Song after song went by, and the surrounding crowd blurred, fading into a background for her performance. When we finally docked and the music stopped, she leaned forward and whispered, "Where do you live?"

"Presidential Towers."

"Over by the Opera?"

I nodded. "Tower Three, 4702."

"I'll meet you there in an hour."

With those words, Aris vanished into the crowd. I tried to follow, but found myself trapped behind a long line of my colleagues, all waiting to the leave the boat. As I filed forward, I saw Aris leave in a black Saab convertible, top down, hair flowing.

I eventually hailed a cab and headed for my apartment with a mixture of anticipation and wariness. I decided to discount Lee's experience with Aris.

Back at Presidential Towers, however, time passed slowly. I became concerned as first one and then two hours passed without Aris. I finally nodded off, only to be awakened by a loud knock.

"Good morning," I said, opening the door to find Aris.

"It's not morning, yet," she said, as her waifish figure slid by me.

I joined her next to the windows. We stood there silently enjoying the lights of the city for some time before she noticed my pictures on the window ledge. Without inquiry, she sat down and began to look at several framed snap shots and two small photo albums. My pictures were mostly of my family and college friends, including Lee and various women I had dated, none of whom had maintained their interest in me for long. When she finished, she held up her hand, and I helped her to her feet.

"Did you learn anything interesting?" I asked.

"You went to the University of Texas from 1988 to 1992. You pledged a fraternity. You've traveled to at least Italy and someplace tropical. You've dated a lot of beautiful women, but no one for very long."

I started to speak, but she continued before I could utter a word. "So you've never been in love?"

"I guess I've never met the right woman." The memories of my repeated rejections reminded me of why I had left Texas.

"All those beautiful southern belles and not a one made your little heart go pitter-patter?" She reached over and patted my chest with her hand.

I forced a smile.

"You're what—twenty-two?" she asked.

"Just turned twenty-three."

"And you've had plenty of chances to fall in love, but haven't. Why not?"

Aris answered her own question before I could speak. "There are a number of possibilities. Perhaps you have some deep-seeded fear of commitment that keeps you jumping from woman to woman. Or maybe you have character flaws that are only evident after someone gets to know you, like your friend Lee."

She turned back toward the pictures and held one up. "No, I should be more generous. Superficial smiles. Perfect makeup. Tell me, Grayson, were they smart enough to recognize your potential?"

I shrugged. "Maybe I was working too hard to give them the attention they deserved."

"But did you ever want it?" she asked as she put her arms around my waist.

"What?"

"Love," she said, moving her mouth just inches from mine.

"Who doesn't?"

She spun away and sat down on my couch, laughing.

"How about you?" I asked, joining her. "Don't you have a boyfriend?"

"Not at the moment."

"Dating?" I asked.

"Intermittently and quietly."

"Like tonight?" I asked, resting my hand on her thigh.

"The law school is rich in gossip, and I like to keep a certain sterile reputation even if the reality is something very different," she said, placing her hand on mine and sliding both up her thigh.

"No man's ever talked?" I recalled Lee's revelation.

"They always find that it isn't in their interest to talk."

"How's that?"

"Perhaps they have a wife or a girlfriend," she said.

"I don't."

"I know, but you'd never talk."

"What makes you so sure?"

Aris tossed my hand back into my lap and her expression turned cold. "Because someone as smart as you would at least find out who I was—"

"Topics and comments editor of the *Review*."

"I'm impressed. You've done your homework, but you're mistaken if you think I trust you."

"You trusted me enough to come to my apartment."

"It's not about trust. It's about incentives."

"Really?" I asked, leaning closer.

"I can help you—or ruin you—in so many ways."

"True," I said, moving my lips toward hers.

"There is one other incentive that I left out," she said, placing both of her hands against my chest and stopping me just short of my intended kiss.

"Yes?"

"By the time I finish with you tonight," she cooed, "you'll have no interest in doing anything that would annoy me in the least bit. If only because you'll be hoping tomorrow morning, when you wake up alone, that I'll come back."

"Will I?"

"Now, shut up and enjoy yourself," she said, sliding down the length of my body and kneeling between my legs.

* * *

Aris was not exaggerating. For three hours, I teetered on the furthest edge of consciousness before finally spending myself to sleep. When I awoke to the buzzing of my alarm clock, I found Aris gone and a note on my bed. "We'll have to get together again." There was no signature.

I lay there, too weak to rise but too excited to sleep, trying to figure out what made Aris so special. All I could come up with was that she experienced life differently, that she pursued each moment of life to its fullest potential. She was right. I had to have this again, and soon.

THREE

I fell asleep again, only to awaken six hours later to a ringing phone.

"Hello," I said, startled.

"I expected you at the library this morning, but I guess you weren't all that interested in seeing me again."

"No. No," I mumbled, still half asleep.

"You were sleeping?"

"Yes."

"It's the middle of the day, for Christ's sake."

"I know."

"Classes begin tomorrow, and I expect you to take them so seriously that even if you don't sleep at all, you go to class and perform like your life depends on it."

"Of course."

"Grayson, I really like you because I can see that you have the same drive that spurred me through my first year. The fun and games of college are over. If you want to become someone great, you have to be willing to pay the price."

"I am."

"Well, then, get with it."

Click.

"Hello? Hello?"

The phone was dead.

In my exhausted state, the whole night still seemed but a dream, and I half expected to suddenly find myself looking out upon the familiar basketball court that had been beneath my bedroom window at the fraternity house in Austin. Only there was the Sears Tower—and Aris's little note. It seemed too good to be true, and I started to feel the creep of arrogance at my success with Aris. Then I remembered how Lee had been blindsided by overconfidence.

I stumbled into the shower, dressed, and drove to the law school, determined to keep my perspective and to avoid Lee's mistakes. Upon arrival, I stole a few furtive glances into the windowless, burned-out tenements behind the law school. I shivered at the proximity of danger that no doubt lurked there and walked briskly inside.

My first stop was the Green Lounge, the designated area to socialize. As I searched the various groupings of students for Aris, I heard no friendly "get to know each other" conversation, only talk of law: "When did you start studying today?" "Did you brief all of the cases for contracts?" "What's the holding of …."

I didn't find Aris.

Seeing my industrious classmates made me realize that I had wasted a good portion of the day. I felt light-headed. My heart was pounding. Classes hadn't even started yet, and I was already behind. Panic-stricken, I headed for the library, climbing the spiral stairway past a hanging oriental carpet and a giant portrait of a ghoulish-looking professor. On the main floor of the library, however, I found every seat occupied. I climbed the stairs to the next floor, continuing my search for a place to begin my future.

As I panned the surrounding stacks of books to get my bearings, my eyes locked on the words "University of Chicago Law Review." I could feel my heart again. The large silver letters labeled a wall in an elevator foyer adjacent to the stairwell. Next to the letters was a windowless wooden door, presumably the entrance to the *Law Review* offices. While I realized that Aris was probably in there, my overriding concern was that I was already behind in the race to become a member of that very institution. My classmates had been working all morning and afternoon; they had at least eight hours on me. So I tore myself away from the shrine and headed off in search of a place to study.

After wandering through towering bookcases, I eventually reached a row of windows overlooking the law school's fountain, the large Midway park, and, about 200 yards across the park, the rest of the gothic university. A long row of two-person tables lined the windows. Every table was filled except for one on my far right, which was tucked into a little notch in the wall. I hurried to it. Once sitting, however, I immediately realized why the table was vacant. I could hear the dull drone of conversations through the adjoining wall.

Seeing as I had no choice, I tuned out the drone and I examined my class schedule for tomorrow: elements of the law, torts, contracts, and civil procedure. Torts, or personal injury law, sounded most interesting. I pulled out the torts book and noticed that it was written by my professor—Rittinger was his name. I wasn't sure whether this was a good or a bad thing, but as there was nothing that could be done, I plunged into the case readings, summarizing as I went along.

An hour or so into my readings, the incomprehensible mumbling became louder, eventually reaching such a clarity that I might as well have been in the same room.

"This shouldn't take long." It was Aris's voice.

My heart quickened with the realization that only a sliver of dry wall separated my table from the *Law Review*'s executive offices.

"No, not at all," said a strange male voice. "I'm ready to get back to editing my Supreme Court clerkship application."

"Not so fast," said another male voice.

"Please," said Aris, sarcastically.

"It wasn't Mr. Gibbs's fault," said the second male voice.

They were talking about Lee.

"Miles, we just can't make exceptions," said the first male voice.

"But Chuckie," Miles said.

"Don't call me that!"

"I'm sorry."

"You know," said Aris, "if we let Gibbs on, we're going to have to readmit Kupow too."

"Well, I'm fairly sympathetic to Kupow's case," said Miles.

"Both Gibbs and Kupow broke the rules," said Aris.

"I know," said Miles, "but these people earned admission under our own strict criteria. Put yourself in their shoes for a moment."

"Undoubtedly, we would be putting both at a disadvantage," conceded Aris, "but I say we make them gain readmission by writing an article."

"Oh sure, they could write flawless fifty-page articles over the next two months, plus study for and attend classes. Not likely," said Miles.

"Oh well," said Chuck.

"I don't have to go along with your positions," said Miles.

There was silence for at least two minutes.

Aris finally spoke. "True. It is, however, long-standing practice for the editor-in-chief to respect the other two votes on the executive board."

Another long silence.

"Assuming Kupow and Gibbs submit their articles for approval at a later date, will you both agree to follow my lead if I find their articles meet our standards?" asked Miles.

"Don't have a problem with that," said Aris. "Chuck?"

"Sure," said Chuck.

The voices stopped, and a door closed. I returned to my reading.

When I had finished, I decided to drive to Lee's apartment to tell him about the meeting. After all, Lee had coached me on the Law School Admissions Test, advised me about law schools, and then helped me with my final applications. I always thought that if I could ever repay him, I would. The least I could do was offer support in the wake of the bad news.

There were few cars out and about on a Sunday night, and I managed to get to Lee's building, between Michigan Avenue's shopping district and Lake Shore Drive, in about twenty-five minutes. I checked in at the front desk and was buzzed through a glass door into the elevator bank. I boarded a waiting elevator, which lurched upward with a squeak. When the elevator opened, I found Lee's door propped ajar with a big law book. I picked up the weighty tome and walked right in. "Lee," I called.

"Hey, come on in." He waved in my direction.

Lee was sitting on the couch with a cordless phone in his lap.

"Expecting a call?"

"Yeah, the *Law Review* board is meeting on my appeal at this very minute."

"I know. That's why I'm here."

The phone rang. "Hello," said Lee, holding an open hand in

my direction to silence me.

There was a pause as Lee listened.

"Oh."

Another pause.

"Tomorrow at lunch. Thank you."

Lee clicked the phone off and turned toward me, his eyes glistening with tears.

"You slept with her, didn't you?"

Before I could figure out what to say, Lee was in my face, shaking his finger at me. "I knew something was going to happen. That little slut!"

I knocked his hand away. "You said you had no feelings for her. I would never have—"

"You're right," said Lee, suddenly regaining his composure. "Just remember, I warned you about her."

"Let's get a beer," I urged.

"No. No. I've got to look over my article outline and print out another copy for the *Review* people."

"You've already got an outline?" I asked.

"Yeah, I've been working on my article since I got the news in August. It's my last chance, and if I fail… ."

"I'm sorry about all this. About the *Law Review*. About Aris."

"Just leave," he said.

I sadly complied.

As I drove back to my apartment I thought about the old Lee who I had all but worshipped in college. During the waning hours of fraternity parties, he would sometimes walk around with a clear plastic cup filled exactly halfway with beer, asking women whether the cup he held was half full or half empty. Whatever the answer, he'd respond with the same stale speech, celebrating the wild, wonderful world. How quickly things can change.

FOUR

I arrived for my first class five minutes early to find all of the seats taken except for a few in the first row. I sat down in the middle of the first row and watched as the last remaining seats were filled by similarly "late" classmates.

I took a deep breath and tried to relax despite the din of seventy-five voices engaged in conversation behind me. Just as I took out my case book and a spiral notebook, a tall, thirty-something, balding man in a suit walked into the room, accompanied by a large German Shepherd. Instant silence.

"Hello. For those of you who may not know me, I'm Professor Bliston. This is my assistant, Bear. Just in case someone might be in the wrong place, this is Elements of the Law."

A small "uh" resonated from the back of the room, and a desperate woman hurried down the steps and then out the door.

"Every year that happens. Anyone else? This is Bliston's Elements of the Law. Leave now or face the prospect of Bear guarding the door."

Bliston panned the room and then began.

"The title for this course, 'elements of law,' lacks a certain self-explanatory nature present in your other classes. Contracts, torts, and civil procedure are all established and coherent disciplines. Even if you're not sure what each of those words may mean, a quick glance in Black's *Law Dictionary* provides an answer. There is, however, no definition in Black's for 'elements of law.' That is because it has no definition."

With those words, my legal career had begun. Bliston rambled on for several minutes about the content of the course before finally arriving at the substance for his lecture. "Let's now start with our first case, *Lochner v. New York*, in particular the famous dissent by Justice Holmes."

As the room echoed with the rush of pages turning to Holmes's dissenting opinion, I was filled with the icy realization that I had just glanced over the dissents. Spots danced before my eyes as I frantically flipped through my materials in search of Holmes's dissent. Finally locating the text, I raced through paragraph after paragraph, trying to grasp his central point, just in case Professor Bliston called on me first. Despite seeing words, even reading words, I could not digest or make sense of them.

"Oh, here's a seating chart," said Professor Bliston, tossing it on the table in front of me. "If everyone could write their name, with phonetic pronunciations of any difficult ones, I would appreciate it. Since I don't know names yet, I shall start with you, fourth row, middle, red sweater."

Reprieve. The spots before my eyes faded, and I was finally able to comprehend full sentences.

"You're probably wondering whether your red sweater had something to do with your being first," said Professor Bliston.

She nodded.

"It did. What's your name?"

"Helen, Helen Lipman."

Just then, I realized that Professor Bliston was climbing up—immediately in front of me—on the table that stretched along the front row, the table where my notebook and case book lay. I managed to rescue my case book just before he sat down with his legs folded together in front of my face.

"Ms. Lipman, could you please tell us what Holmes was so concerned about in his dissent?"

As I went to write Professor Bliston's question into my notes, I realized that his brown wing tip was firmly planted on top of my notebook. I delicately tried to pull it free, but it wouldn't budge.

"Justice Holmes believes that the Constitution is made for people of fundamentally different views," said Lipman, looking up and down from her notes to the professor. "The people of different states, acting through their legislatures, should have the right to enact laws, even if those laws ... well, contradict the policy beliefs of the Supreme Court."

I pulled harder on my notebook. No luck. In resignation, I tried to write around the outline of Professor Bliston's shoe. Because at least a third of my notebook page was taken up by the shoe, I wrote as small as possible.

"Yes," boomed Professor Bliston, flailing his arms above me. "Ms. Lipman, what do you think the New York maximum hour law was trying to accomplish?"

"It was trying to help workers who had to work too many hours."

"How did this law help workers?" asked Bliston.

"Well, people ought not to work such long hours. It's unhealthy," she said, her head still bouncing up and down like a wooden toy between her book and Bliston.

"Ms. Lipman, what if the Illinois legislature passed a maximum hour law for lawyers. 'No lawyer may work more than 2000 hours a year.' Would you like that?"

"Is that a lot of work?" she asked.

The class laughed.

"Ms. Lipman, it amounts to forty hours a week with two weeks of vacation."

"That sounds fair," she answered.

"But what if you were to learn that most lawyers work 2500 hours a year and that associate salaries are based on the assumption that they are working 2500 hours a year?"

"I'm sorry?" asked Ms. Lipman, turning through the pages of her book in search of an answer.

"Do you think that you would get paid the same amount after the statute was passed?"

After a pause, she closed her book and answered, "Well, no."

"That's right, you would be paid at least twenty percent less. The law firm would have to hire more lawyers to maintain their client load, and the additional health benefits would further erode your starting salary. Now, would you like to have the state fix your starting salary?" he asked, pointing in her direction.

"I suppose not."

"Ms. Lipman, who should decide such an issue, the New York legislature or the Supreme Court?"

"It would seem that the legislature would be more representative of the majority's will."

"But Ms. Lipman, isn't the will of the majority just a matter of raw power?"

"Well."

Professor Bliston went on, speaking with greater force: "What is the democratic process but power politics—the powerful exercising their will over the weak, over the minority? What else is a constitution for, or for that matter, the rule of law itself, if not for quelling the strong when they seek to take from the weak?"

This Socratic banter went on for what seemed an eternity before Bliston removed his foot from my notebook, apparently oblivious to the great hardship that he had caused me. He then walked over to the door, grabbed the immense Bear by the collar, and pulled him a safe enough distance so that the students could pass.

"Good day!" he said.

The class burst into conversation, and I looked down at my dirt-smudged page of notes, where tiny lines of text curved around a blank area in the shape of Bliston's shoe. I laughed at my odd start, packed up my books, and headed to the next class. This time I was early enough to find a more comfortable center seat in the fifth row.

When Professor Rittinger arrived, the class fell into complete silence. I looked up to see a raven-haired man with a huge, beaming smile, the biggest I had ever seen.

"Hello, I'm Professor Rittinger and this is torts. From the most essential and basic right—the right to our person—comes the most basic tort: assault. Our first case, *I. de S. and Wife v. W. de S.*, concerns the assault of a barmaid in medieval England. For those of you who have not heard, I call by rows, and today the lucky row is the fifth." There was a barely perceptible yelp from someone to my right.

Rittinger continued, "I'll start on my left, your right ... yes, Mr.?"

"Polinsky."

"Mr. Polinsky, at what time of the day does this assault take place?"

"After the tavern closed. I suppose that it's late at night."

"Why is the time important?"

"The state of mind of I. de S.'s wife."

"Right, people fear the night, particularly during the Middle Ages. Why don't you go ahead and flesh out the details of this case for the class."

"It was dark. The pub was closed. This drunk guy was banging on the door, trying to get some wine. The woman goes to the window to chase him away. She sticks her head out the window—"

Rittinger interrupted, shouting in a high-pitched woman's voice, "Go away ye big brute! Go back to the filthy wormhole from where's you come!" Saliva rained down on the first row.

"Uh," continued Polinsky, "the guy who wanted a drink was angry at the bar hag, maid I mean, so he swung his axe within inches of her head and struck the wall near her head. She subsequently brought suit."

"Yes, Mr. Polinsky, which end of the axe did the man swing at the bar hag?"

"I don't know," said Polinsky.

"Let's try your neighbor. You are?"

"Webster."

"Mr. Webster, do you have an answer to my question?"

"I don't think the opinion says which end of the axe hit the door."

"Correct. What was his swing supposed to accomplish?"

"Revenge for being locked out," said Mr. Webster.

"No. Who's next?"

"Looper," said the man sitting to my immediate right. I noticed that his hands were shaking under the table.

"What was the axe-wielding man trying to accomplish?"

"He wanted to scare her into serving him wine?"

"Correct. Now what's wrong with that?"

"He invaded her personal space?"

"No," said Rittinger, spinning in a circle in apparent frustration.

I realized that I was next.

"Next. Who are you?"

"Grayson Bullock, sir," I said, feeling my own knees begin to shake.

"What was wrong here?"

"He was using force to acquire service," I said.

"Right. What's wrong with that?"

"It would have constituted a kind of theft, where she received no extra payment for having to open and serve this man when she otherwise would have been closed."

"That's right. He swung that big old axe," Rittinger picked up his torts book and slammed it into the first row table, kabam! Everyone jumped. "If this sort of behavior wasn't punished, what would happen?"

"Threats would become fashionable, more common. There would be nothing to deter this sort of one-sided transaction."

"Ideally what should happen in this situation?"

"Well, perhaps the man could offer to pay the barmaid extra since it's so late."

"Exactly," said Professor Rittinger. "There is some amount of money, call it X," he said, drawing a big X on the chalk board, "that the bar maid could be paid to make her indifferent to having to reopen the pub. If the value of a drink to the thirsty traveler is less than X, it is an inefficient transaction and it shouldn't go forward. If it's equal to or greater than X, then the transaction will go forward because the man and the woman will negotiate a price."

"Next. You are?"

Despite feeling like my heart was trying to climb up my throat, I thought that I had handled myself well. The class went on with Professor Rittinger imitating the various characters in each case and calling on person after person, row after row. When the class was finally over, my hand hurt from writing. I was sure that no other human being could speak as fast as Professor Rittinger.

The rest of my classes proceeded on like that, questions and answers, my heart racing and slowing with each round. After my classes were over, I returned to the library and placed a permanent reservation on my favorite table, the one with eavesdropping capability on the *Law Review* offices. The librarian was surprised that I wanted it, warning me that I was likely to be disturbed by the *Law Review*. Given my interest in Aris, that was exactly what I wanted.

FIVE

The rest of first week blurred together with day one. I was utterly exhausted, suffering from eye-strain, and dreaming about the grotesque scenarios from the more sordid cases. Aris hadn't called and though we managed to walk within a few feet of each other on a half-dozen occasions, she had given me no more than a fleeting glance. My luck, however, finally changed on Saturday morning, when there was a knock on my door.

"Hello. Hello," said Aris. She kissed me briefly on the lips and then barged past.

"Good morning," I said, admiring her suede riding pants and trademark snug-fitting sweater. She reminded me of Audrey Hepburn in *Breakfast at Tiffany's*.

"I was wondering whether you would like to accompany me up to Lake Geneva for the weekend?" she asked.

"Switzerland?"

"No, Wisconsin."

"Sure."

Within the hour, we were barreling north on I-94 in Aris's Saab convertible—top up. It was in the thirties, overcast, and drizzling.

"How was first week?" asked Aris.

"The week seemed to last forever. It felt like a month."

"That's because time perception is a product of awareness. Watch this."

Aris whipped the wheel to the left, causing the car to careen onto the shoulder and toward a construction barricade. Everything slowed down. I could see the paint scratches and cracks on the orange construction barrels, even a small pile of sand that had leaked out of a crack in the first barrel. Then Aris brought the car back onto I-94.

"Everything slowed down, didn't it?" she asked, putting her hand on my tense thigh.

"Yes," I said, my heart still pounding.

"Anytime that we can put ourselves in a higher state of awareness, like starting law school—or traveling to a strange place on vacation—time, relatively speaking, moves more slowly."

"But perception is not really time. A minute is still, after all, a minute."

"Of course. While we can't control time itself, we can train ourselves to better appreciate the time we have."

"So is this trip a lesson?"

"You'll just have to see now, won't you?"

During the drive, we talked about what we had done and what we wanted to do. Before I knew it, the cityscape had been replaced by the pumpkin-covered fields and towering golden-leaved woods of rural Wisconsin. The village of Lake Geneva emerged from this countryside as a collection of little row houses containing assorted shops and restaurants. In front of the row houses, the sidewalks and lamp posts were decorated for the season—hay bales, scarecrows, pumpkins, squash, and various streamers in black, orange, gold, and red. We parked on the main street and walked around, grabbing a couple of hot dogs and browsing through the antique shops.

By the time we arrived in our room overlooking the lake, the sun was setting into a gap of clearness between the clouds and the horizon. Aris sat on the edge of the bed, staring out at the orange sky. She pulled her sweater over her head, revealing her bare breasts, perfect circles which flowed seamlessly into the rest of her body. I was overcome by the totality of beauty in her sleek figure, enticing and moving as an entirety rather than in its parts. I lifted her slender legs, removing one boot and then the other. As I tossed the boots aside, she slid her riding pants and panties over her hips. Completely nude, Aris reclined back onto the bed, glowing alabaster in the fading light of late afternoon. Without noticing her move, I felt her all around me, undressing me and pulling me into her.

* * *

I woke up from a post-coital nap to find Aris staring out at the dark lake. She was leaning back in an occasional chair with the soles of her feet pressed against the picture window. Hovering just above the lake was a full moon, which had turned the trees in the distance a ghostly silver.

"I'd be happy to just stay here with you forever," I blurted out.

"They're too many places to see," she said. "Any one place, no matter how splendid, eventually becomes routine."

"Maybe I'm just overwhelmed."

She turned toward me. "Overwhelmed by what?"

"Moving halfway across the country. Starting law school."

"It will pass," she said. "You'd be surprised what you can get used to."

"Even though this is where I've always wanted to be, there's something unpleasant about the atmosphere," I confessed.

"The work?"

"The competitiveness, I think."

Aris glided over to where I was sitting, knelt, and grabbed both of my hands. "It's a little early, isn't it, for disillusionment?"

"I'm not disillusioned. I'm just trying to, as you put it, get used to things."

"The best way to get used to something is to just do it. If you think about it too much, you'll get distracted. That's dangerous."

"How do you stay so focused?" I asked.

Aris looked back toward the lake. "My dad," she said. "My mom died from cancer when I was little, and he never remarried—because he loved her so much. I'm who I am because of him."

I touched her shoulder.

A single tear rolled down her cheek, and she wiped it away. "What made you want to go to law school?" she asked.

"My grandfather was a lawyer and Congressman with great promise before he was killed during World War II. You see, I always thought that law school here, at Chicago, would be the beginning of my ascent to public importance. Like him."

She rested her head against my knee. "If you just keep your focus, it will be."

"How do you do that though?"

She lifted her head and looked up at me. "Has anyone ever explained the grading system to you?"

"Only that it's pretty random."

"It's quite the opposite," she explained. "On each exam, you'll have one to four long factual scenarios of crimes, personal injuries, whatever. You'll have three hours to identify as many legal issues as possible. The exams are then graded blind."

"I've heard all that."

"Well," continued Aris, "every time the professor sees that a student has noticed a legal issue, he makes a little mark, and when he finishes each exam, he adds up the marks."

"But how do those marks correspond to grades?"

"Inevitably, there will be one student who has seen more issues than anyone else. That exam gets the highest grade. Those students with the second highest number of marks get the next highest, and so on. While only one student sees sixty issues, half the class may see fifty-four. Hence, the difference between being a Supreme Court clerk and being average may amount to consistently seeing just a few more issues than the rest of your class."

"That sounds random," I persisted.

"The randomness is merely apparent, an artifact of the intense competition among equals."

"So it's close for everyone?"

"Don't worry, dear Grayson. I'll help you." She sprung up into my lap and embraced me.

As the moon disappeared into the blackening lake, Aris took me inside of her.

SIX

Our weekend together at Lake Geneva was fantastic, and I realized that I was quickly developing feelings for this remarkable woman who shared and understood my dreams. Indeed, when I awoke alone on Monday morning, I felt empty, missing Aris. Fortunately, there was the distraction of law school, which Aris had convinced me to approach with a renewed enthusiasm. She also helped me to understand the competitive nature of the law school. At class on Monday, I saw everyone and everything in a different light: confidence and uncertainty, strength and weakness, courage and fear.

I noticed how the predators among us set out to exploit their classmates' anxiety. If someone mentioned that they weren't studying enough, another would say he'd been working seventeen-hour days. When someone lamented their long hours, another bragged about how he could speed-read and needed only half as much time. If someone complained about not having enough time for their wife or kids, another would suggest that law school was not the place for someone who cared about their wife and kids, noting the near universal divorce rate among married students. Whatever it took to make others uneasy, they did it. But they never talked about these games. At least superficially, everyone pretended to be everyone's friend.

All of this made me realize that, at least at the highest levels of society, one of the crucial differentiating factors between success and mediocrity is one's emotional state, in particular, the ability to quell anxiety. Or in the case of some of my unscrupulous classmates, the ability to produce anxiety in others. I was repulsed by their games and wanted no part of them. I told myself that I would succeed by playing fair, that personal integrity mattered. Yet the exchanges and the intensity of the competition sometimes disturbed me so much that I'd lay awake in bed at night wondering what I was doing here.

With morning, however, I always returned to my senses, or at least to Aris's influence. I would tell myself that to truly make a difference, I had to soar beyond the grading curve, despite my classmates' games. As Aris had explained on the drive back from Lake Geneva, disquietude is hardly confined to the sterile marble of Chicago Law. "Was it easy," she asked, "for Judge Vanderlyden to issue his decision in the Cardenas case when he knew that his safety and that of his family would be placed in jeopardy?" Moral doubt would present itself at every important moment in my life, both public and private. I could not simultaneously live a meaningful life and avoid opaque choices.

Surprisingly, the next two weeks of law school passed without Aris's company, so when the phone rang, I was desperate to hear her voice.

"Hello!"

"Hey, this is Lee." His voice sounded upbeat. "I was just calling to see whether you wanted to have a few beers?"

"Sure," I said.

"I'll meet you at the Berghoff at nine."

When I arrived, Lee was already there, saving a seat on the far left side of the long bar, over by a row of windows. His handsome features were sunken, but the slouch was gone.

"Hey," I said.

"Bartender, bring a beer for my friend," he shouted, pointing in my direction.

Service was immediate, and the beer was good.

"So how are things going?" I asked.

"I'm making good progress on my *Law Review* article, but it sucks that I have to do it this way." Lee stared into his beer.

"How's the job hunt?" I inquired, trying to change the subject.

"That's why I called. Today I accepted an offer from Kirkland's D.C. Office."

"First choice?"

"Oh, yeah, apparently my grades were ample."

"Congratulations," I said, raising my glass in a toast. "Who needs the *Law Review*!"

Lee stopped his glass in midair. "What?"

"Well, you didn't need the *Law Review* after all, did you? I mean … most people would give their right arm to work at a firm like Kirkland."

"You still don't get it," said Lee, slamming his beer down. "No *Law Review*, no Court of Appeals clerkship, no chance at a Supreme Court clerkship, probably no chance of ever becoming a partner at Kirkland."

"You're right, I don't get it. What if your article is rejected?"

"That won't happen," said Lee, shaking his head.

"What are you going to do, kill yourself?" I asked, trying to put things in perspective.

Lee stuck his index finger into the beer and swirled it.

"We're moving into first quarter exams," I continued. "You just can't keep up this pace."

"I can. And I will."

"Look at you. You've lost twenty pounds. You truly look sick."

"I don't care," said Lee. He licked the foam from his finger and then chugged the entire glass of beer.

"I've got a lot of work to do," I said. "I really should be going."

Lee didn't try to stop me. I walked out into the urban canyons of downtown and retreated back to my own apartment, happy to be alone and free from the distraction of Lee's situation.

* * *

I awoke the next morning to my ringing phone.

"Hello," I said.

"Good morning." It was Aris.

"Oh, good morning," I said, sitting up and trying not to sound like I had been sleeping.

"I was just calling to see whether you might be interested in accompanying me to a dinner party on Monday night."

"That sounds great."

"Eight o'clock. The Everest Room. And please, wear your best conservative suit and tie. Judge Vanderlyden will be there."

"Sounds like an intimidating crowd."

"It will be a great opportunity for you to network and make some valuable connections. Judge Vanderlyden is highly regarded by the judiciary and wouldn't be a bad judge to clerk for."

"Sounds good."

"Anything else before I head off to a *Law Review* meeting?"

"No."

"See you on Monday."

"Bye."

Later that afternoon, I powered up the Mac for a little research on the judge. One of the minor perks of being a law student is free, unlimited access to Westlaw, an incredible computerized data base: major and minor newspapers, magazines, legal cases, textbooks, and even public records like property values and tax information. All searchable by any combination of words.

I logged on, entered my password, and watched the Westlaw menu scroll across the screen. I decided to start with newspapers so I entered, "ALLNEWS," and was taken to the newspaper database. At the search prompt, I entered, "Vanderlyden."

"Searching," Westlaw replied.

After about twenty seconds, the screen cleared and took me to my search result: eight articles. The most recent article was from the *Miami Times Herald*, May 9, 1992, "Federal Appellate Court Upholds Death Sentence for Bolivian Killer." I skimmed along quickly. Judge Vanderlyden had penned the opinion upholding Ramon Cardenas's death sentence under the new antiterrorism law. The next six articles concerned the same case. The last article, however, was about Judge Vanderlyden's appointment to the court. It described how Vanderlyden had attended both college and law school at Yale, had clerked for Justice Brennan, and then went straight into academia at Yale Law. His father had been managing partner of Cravath, one of the oldest law firms in New York City. He was, in short, the ultimate insider.

It then occurred to me that Aris's last name, Byrd, was somewhat unusual. The law school directory listed her home as Charlottesville, Virginia, so I entered a new search: "Byrd and

Charlottesville." After about fifteen seconds, one document appeared: *Daily Progress*, Charlottesville, Virginia, March 17, 1992, "Byrd Wins Seat on School Board Despite Controversy." I started reading. Christoph Byrd, millionaire venture capitalist, prevailed in an election to the Albemarle County School Board. The central issue of the election had been the revelation that Byrd had sent his daughter to private boarding school, rather than to the Albemarle County Schools. No surprise there, I thought to myself.

I entered "off" and returned to my studies.

SEVEN

My Monday began with news of the armed robbery of Professor Rittinger over the weekend. The robber had entered Rittinger's law school office with gun drawn, had taken his wallet and Rolex, and then had knocked him unconscious with the butt of the pistol. The Monday edition of the law school's newspaper, the *Phoenix*, explained that this was the first violent crime to take place inside the law school.

I was surprised they had made it this long. The University of Chicago is an island of prosperity resting in a sea of Chicago's most dangerous neighborhoods. The street at the back of the law school is the boundary between the university community and several square miles of urban wasteland that had once been a middle class enclave of apartments and stores. All that was long gone, and the boarded-up buildings were now the playground of gangs and drug addicts from the nearby housing projects.

The newspaper explained that while thefts had been a constant problem—laptop computers tended to disappear the second their owners took their hands off of them—there had been no violence within the institution's hallowed halls. This was probably because after five o'clock, entry into the law school was limited to one door, which was monitored by a security guard who checked student IDs. According to Professor Rittinger, under no circumstances could the armed robber have passed for a student. The *Phoenix* surmised that the robber had entered earlier in the day and had hidden in the library and that he had escaped while the guard was making a general sweep of the first floor, which he did periodically.

I read on in the *Phoenix*. My eyes were immediately drawn to an article entitled "The *Law Review*'s Kupow Affair," authored by a student group, the New Millennium Movement. The piece criticized the *Law Review*, in particular Miles Vanderlyden, for expelling one of its members following her difficult pregnancy. It explained that as editor-in-chief, he had the sole power to suspend the rules in such situations. The article also called on students to join a candlelight vigil that was to be held outside the *Law Review* office at 4:00, which is when the executive board would be hearing Mary Kupow's appeal of her expulsion.

Sure enough, that afternoon, when I went to study in my library carrel, dozens of students were gathered outside the *Law Review* office. Each held a small lighted candle. I hurried by and settled into my desk, ready to overhear Mary's meeting with the Board. The meeting was already underway.

"Here are copies of a letter from my doctor explaining my condition," said Mary. "Not only was I in my last month of pregnancy, but I developed a blood clot in my leg, which in turn threw off smaller clots that eventually lodged in my lungs. I almost died. I couldn't breathe because a clot was obstructing the blood flow to my lungs."

"Mary, we don't contest the gravity of your health problems," said Chuck. "In fact, they're beside the point."

"How can that be? I mean, I would've completed these assignments—"

"Sure," said Chuck, "but the only thing that matters is that you didn't complete your assignments. The rules are unequivocal in announcing that a staff member's failure to complete assignments, for whatever reason, results in the termination of their membership."

"But isn't that draconian?" asked Mary.

"People relied on you."

"You can't discriminate against me because of either my medical disability or because of my pregnancy."

"Of course," said Chuck, "but under the law, you would only have a discrimination case if you met our usual standards and then we terminated you anyway, because of your disability or gender."

"That's correct," said Aris.

"Mary," said Miles, "my concern is that you will remain on

the *Review* without having done as much work as your fellow staffers. After all, the work you missed accounts for about one-third of each member's quarterly workload. Is it fair to your costaffers?"

"That was my next point. I understand that staffers must complete two citation checks."

"Two or three," said Aris.

"I'm willing to do four or five or six, whatever it takes to catch up."

"But then you diminish the amount of cite-checking other staffers will do," said Chuck.

"Yes, but didn't they do my work for me while I was sick?"

"Chuck and I did your work," said Aris.

"Oh."

"To be perfectly honest," said Aris, "it would be impossible for you to do more than one cite check a quarter and still attend classes."

"Yes," said Miles, "cite checks take fifteen to seventeen hours a day for seven to ten days straight. It's the most exhausting task that I've ever had the displeasure of undertaking."

"I bet you're already way behind this quarter," said Aris.

"Have you even been to class?" asked Chuck.

"I'm coming back on Monday."

"You've missed half your classes," said Chuck. "Be realistic. You're going to have trouble just catching up."

"Do you have anything more, Ms. Kupow?" asked Miles.

"No."

"We'll let you know our decision as soon as possible," said Miles.

"Thank you," said Mary, obviously in tears by the wavering tone of her voice.

I returned to my readings only to be disturbed several minutes later by cheering from outside, in the courtyard. Directly below the library, at least fifty students were gathered around Mary, who was giving a speech of some kind. I couldn't make out her words though. When she finished, the crowd began to shout, "Hey, hey, ho, ho, Vanderlyden has got to go!" They repeated the same chant again and again, alternating between Vanderlyden and the *Law Review* until someone screamed, "It's him!"

Sure enough, Miles had been recognized as he tried to leave the building. I watched as Miles walked quickly toward the large Midway park. "Let's follow him," someone from the crowd shouted. A general cheer erupted as they gave chase to Miles, screaming and taunting him in such a cacophony that I couldn't hear what they were saying. Miles's pace immediately accelerated into a jog and then an all-out sprint as he fled from the crowd, eventually disappearing into the maze of gothic quadrangles on the opposite end of the park.

EIGHT

I arrived early at the Everest Room, which was on the fortieth floor of a downtown skyscraper. Seeing no one else, I walked over to the restroom. To my surprise, I found Miles at the sink, rubbing his suit jacket with a wet towel.

"Miles," I said, surprised.

He jumped, looking puzzled, almost scared.

"Oh, I'm sorry," I said, realizing that we had never met. "I'm Grayson Bullock. Aris invited me to join you all this evening."

Miles tentatively shook my hand. "I thought you might be one of the protesters," he said.

I went over to the other basin and as I was checking my tie in the mirror, the stall door behind me opened. A skinny albino figure with pale blue eyes and a pile of curly white hair emerged from its shadowy confines. The hair was anachronistically high, almost like a wig from the eighteenth century.

"So you're Aris's boy ... friend," he said, approaching the basin yet continuing to stare at me.

"Chuck Hellar," he said, turning on the water.

"Grayson Bullock," I said in response.

After Chuck had washed his hands, he pointed to a spot on Miles's back. "You missed a splash of egg," he said.

"I give up," said Miles. "Let's see whether the others are here."

We walked outside and found Aris standing by a window, gazing out over the streetlights below.

"Good evening," I said, admiring her sleek black cocktail dress, which draped off of her shoulders and stopped mid-thigh.

"Ditto," she replied, turning in our direction. "Have you three been here long?"

"No, just a couple of minutes," said Miles.

"You have something on your shoulder," Aris said.

"Please don't remind me," Miles replied.

"There's the Judge," said Aris.

I turned to see a plump man with gray hair coming our way. He seemed friendly, not at all like the stiff scion of establishment New York that I had imagined.

"Son," said the Judge, patting Miles on his shoulder. "What's this?" he asked looking at his hand.

"Egg," replied Miles.

The Judge pulled out his handkerchief. He wiped Miles's suit and his own hand. Then he turned toward Aris. "Miss Byrd, good to see you again," he said, shaking her hand.

"Always a pleasure," said Aris. "I'd like you to meet my friend, Grayson Bullock."

We shook hands.

"Where's my favorite daughter-to-be, Miss Katie Duke?"

"Right here," said Katie, coming out of the women's room.

"Pretty Katie, as usual your parents asked me to send their love," said the Judge, kissing her cheek with obvious pleasure.

Katie was an awkward sight. While her red hair was striking, she was generally unattractive, with a nose that was about twice as large as it should have been and a superfluous thirty pounds. I thought that she had done quite well for herself in catching Miles, an extraordinarily slick and attractive man who could have played James Bond in the movies.

"Chuck, I almost forgot you," said the Judge, shaking his hand.

Chuck looked annoyed.

Two portly men in cheap blazers and clip-on ties walked up behind the Judge. When one of them cleared his throat, the Judge turned.

"Everyone, I would like to introduce you to our security for the evening, Messieurs Kelley and Gonzalez, United States Marshals."

They nodded in unison.

"Are you still having a security problem?" asked Aris.

"Your table is ready, sir," interrupted the hostess.

"Let's avoid such unfortunate topics," said the Judge, "and enjoy an evening of fine food and wine."

Our group followed behind the hostess and the Judge. I was second to last, right in front of Chuck. As we walked toward a large round table by the window, Chuck whispered, "So where has Aris been hiding you?"

"Are you familiar with the women's restroom outside the *Law Review* office?" I whispered.

"Cute," said Chuck, patting my shoulder.

We all took our seats. I managed to end up just to Judge Vanderlyden's left and to Aris's right. Miles, Katie, and Chuck, in that order, were on the other side of the Judge. The two marshals sat at another table.

I found myself unable to take my eyes off of Chuck. He had fine, beautiful features—only he was so pale, translucent even. His strange hair was almost the same white as his skin, a pile of unruly curls that seemed to rise as high from his hairline as his chin was below. I watched curiously as he struggled to free the napkin from its holder while he tried to make small talk with Aris. He was stiff, hesitating before moving and also before talking, like he was about to stutter, though he never did. I also realized from his bony hands that he was too skinny, almost anorexic-looking.

When the waiter came, we all ordered the fixed price dinner for that evening—rabbit pie, mango sorbet, mixed greens, roasted goose, assorted cheeses, and a choice of desserts.

"I've taken the liberty to order some excellent claret, Chateau Mouton 1966," said the Judge.

I didn't know terribly much about wine but I gathered from the sly smile on Chuck's face and the frequent bobbing of his head that this was something quite good—or at least quite expensive.

"So Grayson, what is your editorial position on the *Review*?" asked the Judge.

"Nothing yet, sir. I'm just a first year."

"My, Aris, hasn't anyone ever advised you against robbing the cradle?"

Aris laughed, blushing.

"I detect a hint of an accent in your voice," said the Judge, grabbing my right arm with more force than I would have liked. "Perhaps Texas?"

I couldn't help but smile. "Yes, sir. Houston."

"I've often flown into Houston—on my way down to Brownsville."

"On your way to South Padre Island?" I questioned.

"No, across the border to San Fernando for bird hunting," said the Judge. He released my arm and gestured as if he were holding a shotgun.

"I've hunted there several times myself," I said.

The Judge's face turned red and seemed to tremor with energy. "My, oh, my," he said, patting my shoulder, again with all too much force.

He and I talked about Mexico and told colorful stories through the first three courses. Finally, the Judge leaned toward me. "While I would love to talk about Mexico all night, I fear that I'm boring my only child, so please excuse me while I attach myself to him."

Aris placed her hand on my thigh, and I turned to hear her whisper, "Fantastic charm job on the Judge. He's liable to adopt you if you're not careful."

Aris stood up and excused herself for a trip to the ladies' room. Shortly after her departure, I felt warm breath on my left ear. I turned, finding my mouth a few inches from Chuck's lips. He was way too close, leaning toward me, his pile of white hair casting a shadow over my face.

"Do you know who Stephanie Stinler is?" he asked.

"Haven't a clue," I said, trying to back away.

"She's last year's *Law Review* topics and comments editor, liberal, clerking for an equally liberal Court of Appeals judge. Well, about two weeks ago, she received a Supreme Court clerkship. Quite unfortunate. Anyway, I got this splendid idea when I heard the bad news ... so I called up an old friend who's now clerking on the Supreme Court and had him acquire some stationary from her justice's chambers. I then dictated a letter to my friend over the phone: "Dear Ms. Stinler. I regret to inform you that I must rescind my offer of employment for a 1993-94 clerkship. Proprietary information has come to my attention that precludes you from serving on my staff. I sincerely apologize that this information was not brought to my attention before extending an offer of employment."

"You didn't," I said, horrified.

"We even had the signature down right. Anyway, before we sent it, we wanted to make sure that someone would be around to stop her from actually calling the justice. You could imagine, of course, how he might not appreciate being an involuntary party to such a practical joke. Anyway, it turns out that another friend of my accomplice was Stinler's coclerk. He agreed to watch Stinler open her letters every day so he could stop her from telephoning the justice. According to accomplice number two, when Stinler received the letter, she read it twice, and then broke into tears. Accomplice number two comforted her for an hour, during which time Stinler explained that they must have found out about her drug use at Berkeley. Then, just as Stinler picked up the phone to call, her coclerk told her that it was all a joke."

"That's awful," I said.

"I know," said Chuck, cackling.

I felt his spittle hit my cheek, and I backed further away. I looked into his blue eyes, trying to determine whether he was laughing at me for believing his story or whether he had really done it and was still reveling in his mischief.

"So what do you think of Mary, Mary, Quite Contrary?" asked Chuck.

"Mary Kupow?" I asked.

"Of course."

"Sympathetic to her plight yet thoroughly annoyed with all the egg-tossing barbarians who have taken up her cause."

"Why are you sympathetic?" asked Chuck.

"She couldn't control her health problems."

"Yeah, but she chose to get pregnant. She had to know that being pregnant could interfere with her *Law Review* duties."

"Well, I suppose it was actually the complications that interfered," I said.

"True, but some significant percentage of pregnancies have complications. She knew that too. She assumed that risk too."

Aris finally returned, and Chuck shrank back into his chair.

The rest of the dinner was pleasant, and I found that Chuck could even be entertaining, provided he was at a safe distance. I actually got the impression that he liked me. As for Katie and Miles, they both seemed completely normal. The only question I had about them was whether they were victims of an arranged marriage by their overbearing families. When all was said and done, Aris was sufficiently pleased with my performance that she invited me back to her place, for the first time.

* * *

As we drove down Lake Shore Drive, Aris explained how Miles, Chuck, and she had inherited their adjacent apartments from older members of the Edmund Burke Society, a respected University of Chicago institution known most for its raucous, parliamentary-style debates. For several years, conservatives had passed on the Hyde Park apartments, which were a few blocks from the university, to the three most influential members, usually *Law Review* editors. Each of the apartments had an apropos name: hers was the Reagan Room; Miles's was the Goldwater Room; Chuck's was the Churchill Room. She explained how each of the living rooms had the appropriate photo framed above the fireplace.

When we exited from Lake Shore Drive onto Forty-seventh Street, I could feel the muscles in my neck tense up. Hyde Park, particularly away from the University, was creepy at night. The streets were dark, and homeless people wandered in and out of the shadows and gathered around barrels filled with burning trash.

We eventually turned down a dark alley lined with dumpsters and the crumbling backs of four-story walk-ups. Cars were parked and double-parked, so that the Saab could hardly negotiate the narrow passage, which was alive with parties of rats sprinting back and forth across our headlights. Aris, apparently familiar with the routine, didn't slow down until we were lodged between two dumpsters.

"We're here," she said.

We climbed rickety wooden stairs to the second floor, then

entered an unlit foyer, and climbed an interior stairwell to the third floor.

"That's Chuck's place, and Miles lives there," said Aris, pointing to the first two doors that we passed in the hallway.

About ten yards up the hall, Aris took out her keys and began unlocking half a dozen locks on her door.

After a considerable push, her heavy steel door swung open. "Home sweet home," she said, turning on the lights. "Not the best address in Chicago, but it is an honor to secure these living quarters, not to mention the convenience to the law school."

We walked into a living area filled with antiques and mahogany moldings. There was a framed, signed photo of President Reagan above the fireplace, and two paintings on opposing walls, a landscape of rolling green hills and a portrait of a man wearing a suit.

"That's my dad," said Aris, pointing to the portrait.

"This is really beautiful."

"Wait until you see the bedroom." She pulled me by the hand through another door and hit the lights. "What do you think?"

A canopy bed in the middle of the room was the only piece of furniture—except for a carved-wood oriental screen that was pushed up against one wall. The other three walls were each adorned with a single painting—two nudes of a petite woman not unlike Aris and one of a man, standing in an old-fashioned bathtub.

"Very nice."

"Go in my bathroom, over there," she said, pointing to an open doorway, "and change into the robe and boxers hanging on the back of the door. Don't come out until I call you."

Behind the door hung a green paisley silk robe and a matching pair of boxer shorts. It was disconcerting to see dry cleaning tags pinned to both. Nonetheless, I followed Aris's instructions and changed into garments that had obviously belonged to one of her former lovers.

"I'm ready," I said.

"Not yet," Aris responded.

When she finally said, "Come on out," I exited the bathroom to find Aris reclining on the bed. She was wearing only a pair of white stockings and a garter belt. It could have been another century, and as I slipped through the canopy into her arms, it was nice to think that prior times were simpler, even if they were not.

NINE

The next afternoon Chuck cornered me in the hallway at law school after classes and invited me to that evening's debate of the Edmund Burke Society. I followed him across the Midway park to the International House dormitory, where we found a sign reading, "Burke Society, upstairs in Home Room." At the top of the stairs, I could hear voices emanating from twin oak doors.

We went inside and crept into the far left end of a long rectangular room. In the center of the room, two antique arm chairs were separated by a small coffee table. A clear area just in front of the chairs, say five yards by five yards, was boxed in by three ragged couches. Beyond the couches were various folding chairs set up in rows. At the far right end, opposite where I was standing, an elaborate bar displayed dozens of wine and liquor bottles.

The attendees, about thirty, half in suits, half in khakis with check or plaid sport jackets, were spread about. Some sat on the couches, others stood in a dense little beehive around the bar.

Chuck pulled me over to the bar and poured both of us a glass of red wine. Without warning, the crowd around the bar moved to fill the empty couches and seats. I followed Chuck, and we took our seats in folding chairs on the periphery.

Two sharply dressed men sat down in the two armchairs. They wore nearly identical gray suits with maroon patterned ties. The one to my left was holding a leather volume while the other had a gavel. The one with the gavel clicked it twice on the coffee table. Silence ensued.

"Welcome one and all to the forty-seventh caucus of the ancient and honorable Edmund Burke Society. Will the secretary please read the minutes from the last caucus."

The secretary read from the leather book. "The forty-sixth caucus of the ancient and honorable Edmund Burke Society last debated the following topic: resolved, this society prefers the arts over science. A speech was called for in the affirmative, and Mr. Ingram argued that aestheticism constitutes the highest good."

A clicking, which I ascertained was the snapping of fingers, filled the room. Without thinking, I instinctively joined in.

"A speech was called for in the negative, and Mr. Hellar accepted. Aestheticism is emotionalism, Mr. Hellar argued, and emotionalism is weakness. He quoted generously from Nietzsche."

A low hiss rose from those seated around us.

"Now, now," said Chuck, quieting the crowd.

"Mr. Vanderlyden took the side of the affirmative. He argued that art, whether it be literature or painting, best captures love, and that when all is said and done, what we remember are those whom we have loved and those who loved us.

"Miss Byrd then took the negative, contending that love is overrated and constitutes nothing more than a small-scale war between two people. Science, she explained, has enabled warfare to rise to a much more glorious scale—where the United States dominates the world."

Fingers snapped. While I reluctantly joined in, I could not escape the imagery of Aris lobbing grenades in my direction.

The secretary then went on to describe speech after speech before finally calling the resolution for the evening's debate: "resolved: good riddance, Mr. Bush." The Secretary then closed his book and turned toward the chairman.

"The chairman will now entertain a speech in the affirmative," he said, sweeping the gavel from left to right across his field of vision.

I noticed only one hand go up.

"Mr. Anthony Paglia," said the chairman.

Anthony Paglia, a short fellow with black hair, stood up and walked into the little hot box between the chairman and the couches. With his back to the chairman, he addressed the center of the audience. "Politicians are like rats. Rats I tell you," he said, squinting his eyes and twitching his nose, and looking quite like a rat himself.

"They should be treated accordingly. That means that the

rules of behaviorism must apply. When they do as voters wish, politicians should be rewarded with contributions and reelection. When they do otherwise, they should be punished and tossed out of office. Fortunately, politicians differ slightly from rats in that they possess the capability, most of them anyway, for analogical reasoning. By this, I mean that a politician who is contemplating breaking from the wishes of his constituents can look around him and see what has happened to other politicians who broke their promises.

"Thus, if politicians routinely break their promises and routinely depart from the wishes of their electorate—without any obvious negative consequences," he shouted, bouncing slightly with each word, "politicians will be more willing to do so. Similarly, if politicians who part ways with their constituencies are routinely booted from office, future politicos will be less likely to do so. Thus I reiterate. One, politicians are rats," he said, making the rat face and twitching his nose again. "Two, rats respond to behavior modification. Therefore, politicians will respond to behavioral modification. Now, one and all, go out next Tuesday and send a message to all politicians by saying good riddance Mr. Bush!" He scurried off and took a seat on a couch.

"For the negative," said the chairman, pointing his gavel toward the distant doorway, "the editor-in-chief."

As Miles Vanderlyden walked slowly from the far edge of the room, the crowd parted to let him pass. He took the floor amid a barrage of clicking. Being a staunch supporter of President Bush myself, I eagerly clicked away.

Miles stood facing the crowd for a couple of minutes before the clicking finally subsided.

"Mr. Paglia simply neglects to consider that most important of conservative principles: loyalty!" he boomed, gripping the lapels on his tweed jacket and pacing slowly to the left across the hot box. "President Bush was the number two man in the Reagan Revolution. He's served our cause for at least twelve years as either president or vice president. And right now, he's our president. To abandon him now, over a small tax increase meant to balance the budget, would be tantamount to disloyalty," he said, turning in the opposite direction.

"While I want Republicans to control Congress, there are certain limits that conservatives place on the means used to achieve our ends. We don't eliminate our leaders to facilitate political gain. It is simply wrong. We should not become Macbeths, forever covered with the blood of our leaders, forever haunted by what we have done to them," he said, reaching the opposite end of the box and turning again.

"Whoever succeeds to the reigns of power next becomes paranoid because the same means could just as easily be used against him. Ultimately, the result is that our leaders' energies will be spent on internal purges—constant rear-guard defensive actions against insurrections—instead of furthering our cause," he said, stopping dead center and turning back toward the crowd. "Didn't anyone's stomach turn at the analogy of President Bush, our leader, to a rat?" he asked. In the long pause that followed, I could see heads nodding throughout the room. "Mine sure did. Such dehumanization is more reflective of moral relativism than of conservatism. Even if we lose, let us lose fighting, fighting faithfully for our leader," he boomed, finally releasing his lapels. "Thank you, mister chairman."

"The pleasure was mine," said the chairman. "Will the editor yield to questions?"

"Two."

"Ah, the junior editor," said the chairman, pointing to Chuck.

Chuck stood up. "Surely, the gentleman doesn't regard loyalty as an absolute virtue. What of criminal activities? What of the Nazi death camps? Surely there are times when we must abandon our leaders?"

"This is not one of those times."

"Why not?"

"Because the President did what he believed needed to be done for the good of the country—"

"But didn't Hitler and many others believe that they were doing what was best for their country? That begs the question of whether it was right."

"Seeing that two questions have been asked and answered, the editor-in-chief is dismissed," said the chairman.

"Thank you," said Miles.

"Is there a second speech in the affirmative?" asked the chairman.

Chuck's hand shot up.

"Ah, et tu Brute?" said the chairman.

Chuck walked pensively across the floor with his chin up. When he reached the middle of the room, he turned back toward the crowd and took a restless deep breath.

"The illustrious Mr. Vanderlyden's call for loyalty is inapposite here," he said, taking another deep breath. "President Bush betrayed our loyalty first by breaking a solemn promise made to each and everyone of us not to raise taxes. Loyalty is, after all, a two-way street. President Bush made us certain promises, and we in turn owed him our support. Once he broke a promise, he became disloyal, and accordingly, we owed him nothing more," he said, turning toward Miles. Chuck tilted his head downward so that the top of his head and his hair pointed at Miles. Everyone looked at Miles, who now sat expressionless on the center couch.

"But beyond that," said Chuck, tossing his head back and regaining the crowd's attention, "loyalty is merely one of numerous competing values that conservatives must weigh each and every day. Certainly loyalty cannot be trampled upon like it has no value, but there will necessarily be occasions when loyalty must come second to some superior value. I call this gathering's attention first to Nazi Germany. You are the supervisor of a concentration camp during the last days of the war. You receive orders to exterminate the 50,000 Jews under your control. What to do? Kill 50,000 Jews or become disloyal? I think that Nuremberg and the universal disgust with the first choice was ample to illustrate that loyalty is best sacrificed in such instances.

"Ah, example number two, the century before the birth of Christ. The Roman Republic is on the verge of collapse. Julius Caesar is consolidating power and subverting the cherished Republican institutions. He is not only your leader but also your friend. Yet you realize that the only chance remaining for the Republic is his assassination. Do you kill your friend or allow him to become dictator and destroy liberty?

"Number three. You are the leader of a bunch of colonists

on a distant shore. Your mother country has taxed the hell out of you and ignored your pleas. Do you remain a loyal citizen, paying your taxes to your illustrious king, or do you lead a revolt, a revolt for liberty and control of your own destiny? What do you do?

"Loyalty is by no means always superior. There are times when the exigency of the moment demands sacrificing values one loves for values that one loves even more. Next Tuesday is no different. I surrender the floor," said Chuck, strolling off the stage.

A general din of conversation rose up about the room after Chuck's speech, and most everyone was staring at Miles again. He stood up and walked to the back of the crowd.

The chairman pounded his gavel, "Order. Order." This helped marginally and enabled the chair to select some other speaker who droned on about the history of loyalty.

I watched the new speaker for a few minutes until I noticed that Aris had arrived. She was standing with Miles and Chuck by the door. Aris caught me staring and waved me over. I got up and joined them.

"Good evening," said Aris.

"Quite an exchange," I said.

"That's what debate is all about," said Miles, trying to force a smile.

"Most certainly," said Chuck, beaming with victory.

"The Society inevitably generates some such exchange every debate," said Aris. "One could hardly call it unusual."

Chuck smiled, and Miles bit his lip.

"Next Tuesday, we're having an election party over at the triplex," said Aris, bouncing up and down ever so slightly.

"A wake," corrected Miles.

"Anyway, at about six, we're going to watch the election returns and barbeque burgers."

"Sounds great," I said.

"You better be there," said Aris.

"I will."

The main door to Home Room suddenly burst open and slammed against the wall with a loud thud.

Everyone turned to look. Even the speaker stopped in mid-sentence.

A man in a gray overcoat fell forward, landing just a few feet from where I stood.

Miles rushed to the man and rolled him over. I recognized him as one of my classmates, Noonan.

"I've been stabbed," said Noonan, holding up his bloody hand.

"Call an ambulance," yelled Miles.

Aris, Chuck, and I, along with dozens of others, gathered around Miles and Noonan. Miles pressed his hands over the bleeding wound in Noonan's gut, trying to stop the blood flow.

Within minutes, an ambulance arrived, and they took over. The crew hoisted Noonan up onto a stretcher and rushed him to the hospital.

The chairman exercised his gavel. "Order. Order."

Miles raised his hand.

"Yes, Mr. Vanderlyden, do you have a motion?"

"I move that we end this caucus without a vote in respect for the injuries sustained by Mr. Noonan."

"Any objections? Seeing none, this caucus is hereby adjourned. The chair advises all to travel home in groups."

Miles, Chuck, Aris, and I waited there for the police to arrive.

TEN

Over the next week, the campus was pensive. Everyone was relieved that Noonan had survived the mysterious stabbing by a hooded mugger, but it was the clearest message yet that students were vulnerable. The election week edition of the *Phoenix* contained numerous articles on Noonan's stabbing and the recent crime wave.

The headline story, however, just below the election day banner, read in bold print: "Deans Put Pressure on *Law Review* Board." The article explained that on Sunday evening, Dean Simpson and Dean of Students Wolf met with Miles, Chuck, and Aris to tell them that they thought Mary should be kept on the *Review*. The article then went on to explain how, under the *Review*'s own rules, the decision was ultimately up to Miles. A quotation from a New Millennium member even referred to him as "Führer Vanderlyden." The article also mentioned that the *Law Review* is a self-funding journal that, for all practical purposes, is independent of the law school. Dean Wolf concurred: "Technically we can't order them to do anything."

I stood up and went to the library, which was completely dark at this early hour. But the door was open so I walked upstairs to my cubicle.

No sooner did I start to read than a door slam echoed from the *Law Review* offices.

"Damn you, Miles," I heard Chuck shout through the wall.

"Public opinion has turned on us," said Miles. "Even the deans think we've gone too far."

"Do you remember what the last chief told you when he picked you as his successor in exchange for your daddy giving his wife that clerkship?" asked Chuck.

"I don't know what my father may or may not have done."

The door slammed again, and silence ensued.

The rest of the day was routine, and by four o'clock I was bored with the law, so I decided to head over to Aris's to help her with the election-wake preparations.

I parallel parked on the street and walked up to the main door, which was held open by a brick. I went inside and ascended the stairwell to the third floor, where I saw Chuck walking out of Aris's doorway with a big smile on his face.

He seemed surprised to see me. "Grayson?"

"Hey, Chuck, I came over to see whether you all needed any help preparing for the party."

"Why don't you come on with me, and I'll show you what you can do."

Chuck gently grabbed my arm and pulled me toward his apartment. As soon as I started moving in his direction, he released me.

He opened three locks and pushed his door open.

"Welcome to the Churchill Room," said Chuck.

Above his fireplace was a photograph of Sir Winston himself.

"What can I do to help?"

"In a minute, Miles is going to arrive with the burger meat. Then you can start making patties."

"So there's nothing I can do right now?"

"Nothing other than keep me company," said Chuck. He put his arm around me.

"Look, I'm going next door," I said, freeing myself from Chuck's grasp and escaping into the hallway.

I knocked on Aris's door as Chuck watched from his doorway.

"Chuck, leave me alone. I'm trying to get ready," Aris yelled from inside. She opened the door wearing a white silk robe.

"Hi," I said, walking right in and shutting the door.

She put her arms around me, stopping me in the foyer. "Nice to see you."

I couldn't help but kiss her lips, and she reciprocated with an open mouth for a few seconds before breaking away.

"Just be quiet now," she said, then knelt before me and unzipped my khakis.

After about five minutes of basking in Aris's enthusiastic warmth, it became obvious that she intended not just foreplay but the end itself. "I want to be inside of you," I said.

She slid her mouth off of me and lay back against the hardwood floor, her knees bent slightly.

I climbed on top of her and moved as slowly as possible, relishing every tingle.

"Just a few seconds more," said Aris, pushing herself against me and rendering my own restraint pointless. As we quivered together, I whispered, "I love you."

"Me, too," she replied, still shaking.

I realized that I needed to avoid spilling anything on my pants so I got up and hurried into her bedroom.

"Hey, where are you going?"

"To the bathroom."

Aris was right behind me, placing her arms around me, trying to stop me.

Just inside the doorway to her bedroom, something caught my eye on her unmade bed … a large wet spot.

"Did you spill something?" I asked.

"No … what makes … you think that?"

"There's something on your bed," I said, pushing her away.

I ducked inside the canopy. The bed reeked of fresh sex.

I looked at her, feeling nauseated.

"It's nothing," she said, placing her hands on her hips.

"It's Chuck, isn't it?"

She scratched her belly and then nodded.

I didn't know what to say.

"I don't have feelings for him," she said.

"What about my feelings? You just told me that you love me."

"I do. Chuck doesn't change that."

"Was this the only time?"

"Why does it matter? What we have isn't diminished by my relationship with Chuck," she said, coming to my side and hugging me.

"Why do you need him when you have me?"

"It's not just me. There's Chuck to think of as well."

"Excuse me?" I said, breaking her embrace and tucking my shirt back in.

"He has no one else."

"Perhaps he should go out and find someone else."

"It's not easy for him," she said, hugging me again.

"That's his problem, isn't it?" I pulled away and started toward her door.

"And mine. And yours!" she screamed behind me.

I stopped with my hand on her doorknob and turned. "Now, how is that?"

"Chuck can do things," she said, holding her hands out to me, palms up.

"Oh, really," I said, feeling dizzy.

"Last week, I suggested that I not see him anymore. He threatened to tell you."

"Well, that's one less blackmail lever that he has to pull. What else does he have on you?"

"Just trust that it's enough."

"I've got to get some air," I said, opening her door. It slammed shut behind me, and I heard her turn the lock.

Outside, I leaned against the wall. My chest and stomach burned, and I thought about my long list of relationship failures, of which Aris was only the latest.

I wanted to leave, but I wanted some answers first so I went back up the hall to Chuck's door. As I knocked, I tried to catch my breath but couldn't.

Chuck opened the door, beaming.

"Is the meat here yet?" I asked, trying to maintain my composure.

"In the kitchen. Want to give me a hand?"

"Sure."

I walked into the kitchen, where there was a huge pile of hamburger meat on the counter.

"Just make them about that size," said Chuck, pointing to a small stack that he had already finished.

"Sure," I said, dipping my hands into the gooey ground meat. I formed it into patty after patty.

"So, are you two in love yet?" asked Chuck.

"No," I said.

"She's fun though, isn't she?" His skinny head bobbed in agreement before I could answer.

"How would you know about that?" I asked.

"I can just tell, you know, by the way she walks, looks at men. She oozes sex."

I took a deep breath. Then I said, "I know about you and Aris."

Chuck's head flew back in surprise, but he quickly regained his composure. "So, I suppose you know that I had her five minutes before you did."

"Are you in love with her?" I asked.

"No." He looked down at the hamburger meat.

"No feelings whatsoever?" I asked.

"You need to understand that our relationship is strictly symbiotic, based on mutual need."

"Well, she no longer needs you."

"But I still need her," he said, kneading the ground beef with some force.

"What do you have on her?" I asked.

"What did she tell you?"

"Nothing."

"Then nothing it is."

I didn't know what to say.

"Gray, I like you. I think you're a smart guy with a brilliant future. I'd bet that you're going to make the *Review*. You'll apply for the best clerkships. Look, I can help you. Aris can help you. Don't make things difficult for me ... or... ."

"Or what?"

"You'll regret it," said Chuck. In my dizziness, his strange hair seemed to rise and threaten, like a cobra spreading its hood.

"So you're asking me to stay away from Aris?"

"No. No. No. Spend time with her, just don't monopolize her."

"Share her, you mean?"

"I'm not going to try to take her away from you, and I presume that you'll grant me the same courtesy."

"I don't see how I have anything to do with Aris's choice of partners."

"Just don't try to convince her to shut me out," Chuck spat, leaning toward me, now inches from my face.

I looked past him at his hand. The hamburger was squirting out between his knuckles.

"I'm not sure that I want to share her," I said. "I may just let you have her."

"Don't be stupid," said Chuck, raising a bloody finger into my face. "That would make my life difficult because she'd be forced to pick between us. You know full well that she'd choose you."

I shrugged.

"Well, perhaps I'm making it too complicated. Allow me to make myself clear. If she shuts me out, I'm going to blame you. Something might happen to your *Law Review* application," he said, tossing a handful of meat into a nearby trash can.

I thought of Lee's affair with Aris and what had happened to his application. "Are you implying that you've done this before?"

Chuck smiled.

I understood. "So, you're going to continue to have a sexual relationship with Aris, and I must do the same if I ever want to...."

"I think you've got it now."

I left him there with the raw meat and walked outside, passing street after street until I reached the lakefront. There I stood alone on a point of rock as waves crashed all around me amid the whipping wet wind. I was awash in pain, the sort of pain that obliterates senses and thoughts and leaves one hollow. I wished that I would have found Aris dead rather than discover that her favors were shared with another. At least, in the grief of her death, I could have idealized her and maintained the illusion of our love.

ELEVEN

For the rest of the week, I screened my calls. But if either Aris or Chuck had called, neither bothered to leave a message. On Thursday, I received an invitation to my old fraternity's Fall Formal that had been forwarded from my Austin address. I thought that it would be a nice diversion from the oppressive weight of Chicago and Aris, so by Saturday afternoon I was back in Austin in search of happier, simpler times.

Nothing had changed at the red brick and white columned mansion. There was a basketball game going on in the yard, and the most beautiful women on campus were lounging around the common areas on the first floor.

Walking into the main living room, I was overcome by the house's familiar fragrance—a blend of sex, sweat, expensive perfume, and beer. It was like I had never left.

"Gray!" yelled Jamie, who had been elected pledge master at the end of the last term.

"Hey," I said, exchanging a seriously hard handshake. Other than having put on a few more pounds around the waist, he was the same red-haired, freckled sadist that I had last seen at my graduation party in May.

"You didn't quit law school, did you?" he asked, punching my arm.

"No, I just wanted a change of scenery."

"Let me get you a Shiner," he said.

"Thanks."

I followed him to the keg taps in the kitchen.

"Big glass or little cup?" asked Jamie.

"Big glass."

Jamie grabbed a forty-four ounce mug with the fraternity

crest engraved in its side and filled it full of Shiner Bock, a rich chocolate-colored brew.

Jamie and I walked back into the living room and kicked a couple of pledges off of a leather couch. I realized that the entire room was full of pledges and women. Of course, I didn't know any of the pledges, but I recognized most of the women. A gorgeous sophomore, Liz, caught my eye. Golden-haired. Miss U.S.A. beautiful. Shallow.

"Pledge dates?" I asked.

"Got to get them hooked."

"Ah, the days of being a pledge. Arranged dates, arranged sex, arranged parties. Not much to think about," I said.

"Except for the male bonding or," Jamie lowered his voice to a whisper, "hazing."

"It was never that bad," I lied, recalling being dropped off naked in the middle of campus.

"Maybe for you," said Jamie, "but you were the asshole who took me on the roof, told me to tie a string to the end of my penis, handed me a brick tied to the other end of the string, and told me to throw the brick off of the roof."

"That wasn't me."

"Are you sure?"

"I never hazed anyone. It was Lee Gibbs."

"You're right. Now there was one cruel son-of-a-bitch."

I shrugged.

"Hey, you want to turn over a new leaf and help me haze a pledge?"

"Why don't we play some basketball?"

"Oh, Gray, come on. It's a new ritual I came up with. I use broken glass." Jamie rubbed his hands together in obvious excitement.

"Is this really necessary?" I pleaded.

"It's going to happen with or without you."

As much as I despised hazing, I wanted to make sure that Jamie didn't get carried away, particularly with something dangerous like broken glass. "I'll observe, but that's all."

"You, Mikowsky," said Jamie, pointing to a little guy whose face was girl-pretty.

"Come with us!" Jamie shouted.

I reluctantly followed Jamie and Mikowsky down the stairs into our basement, fully prepared to intervene if an injury appeared imminent.

"Take off your clothes," said Jamie.

Mikowsky hesitated.

"Now!"

He stripped and threw his clothes on a table covered with wine glasses and broken pieces of wine glasses.

Jamie grabbed a chair from the table and placed it in the middle of the room.

"Get on the chair!" shouted Jamie.

Mikowsky sat on the chair.

"No, stand on it!" Jamie yelled.

He crouched on the chair.

Jamie went behind him and tied a black blindfold around his eyes.

"Stand all the way up." Jamie slapped his rear.

Mikowsky complied.

Jamie picked up a piece of the glassware and brought it to Mikowsky. "Do you feel this?" he asked, rubbing it against his left hand.

"Yeah," Mikowsky said.

As soon as Jamie jerked it away, he turned on a high resolution tape. The room echoed with the sound of breaking glass. With each shatter, Mikowsky shook ever so slightly. His privates shriveled up, shrinking more and more until he truly looked like a girl.

Jamie quietly spread potato chips around the floor near the chair. I was relieved that the ritual was of a psychological nature.

The tape ended.

"Jump!" ordered Jamie.

"But—" said Mikowsky.

"Jump by the count of three or you're out!" shouted Jamie. "One … two … ."

Mikowsky jumped with his hand over his crotch and landed in the chips. He rolled to his side.

"I'm cut," he moaned.

Jamie pulled the blindfold off to reveal a couple of tears.

"Chips," said Mikowsky, thoroughly relieved.

"Get dressed and clean up," said Jamie.

Mikowsky scuttled about, his clothes in his hands.

"He was really scared," said Jamie, laughing. "Speaking of fear, you should see the pledge in the dungeon."

"How long has he been there?"

"Two days."

"Are you nuts? That's way too long."

"Then you can let him out," said Jamie.

We opened a closet that led to our so-called dungeon.

When the mansion was built back in the 1950's, the builders discovered a small limestone cave running down at a forty-five degree angle from the basement. Initially it was used as a wine cellar, but as time went on and sadism became more popular among fraternities, the cave was transformed into a dungeon, complete with three sets of shackles.

Jamie grabbed a flashlight at the cave's entrance, and we descended into the nastiest smell—a musty concoction of urine and feces. We both covered our noses.

"Mr. Williams, your pardon has been granted," said Jamie.

The flashlight shone on a dirty nude body shackled to the wall. The body used its shackled wrists to shield its eyes.

Jamie pulled out some keys and undid the locks.

"Your clothes are in the basement closet. Get out of here before I change my mind," he said.

We followed Williams back up to the basement. "Shall I get you a date?" asked Jamie.

I smiled, amazed that only one year ago I was part of all of this nonsense.

"How's Liz?" Jamie asked, bringing me back from my thoughts. "I saw you staring at her earlier, and she's asked about you several times."

"Really?" I said, surprised that she even remembered me.

"I'll go have a word with her. Why don't you get your stuff."

When I returned with my suitcase, Jamie and Liz were already waiting.

"Hi Gray," she said, hugging me gingerly.

"Good to see you again," I lied.

We walked across the street to her condo, where we drank and chatted for a couple of hours, changed clothes, and ordered a pizza. At the scheduled hour, we joined the party at the fraternity house. A band played the usual litany of college rock, from the Cure to the Violent Femmes. Liz was a pleasant distraction from the realities of my life, and she looked stunning in her black party dress. When the band finally quit for the night, we stumbled back to her condo.

Once in her bedroom, we kissed and groped, managing to undress each other despite our mutual state of intoxication. Liz reclined back on the bed and spread her legs with the lackadaisical ease indicative of a common and mundane undertaking. As I climbed on top of her, I couldn't help but think of Aris.

"I'm seriously involved with someone else," I said suddenly, unsure of any other way to remove myself from the moment.

"Oh," said Liz, as she closed her legs and rolled sideways. "Who is she?"

"Her name's Aris. We met in Chicago."

"That's nice."

"I'm sorry."

"Me, too," she said.

We were sufficiently tired and drunk that we fell asleep as we lay there together.

* * *

The next day, while I was waiting for my plane, I thought about the kind of life that I wanted. There was something to settling down and marrying a woman like Liz. She had to be reasonably smart to get into UT, and I would imagine that her apparent shallowness was not a matter of genetics but rather a learned trait. And shallowness isn't all that bad. After all, a beautiful, complacent wife had to be worth something. For a few moments, I really thought that I wanted to marry someone like Liz, return to Texas, and live quietly ever after in my own corner of the world. We'd have beautiful kids, lots of built-in friends, and UT football games to attend every fall.

But my thoughts quickly returned to Aris. I was hooked on Aris and her world, a world where I could be a real player, writing important opinions on the Court of Appeals, maybe even the Supreme Court, eventually running for public office. Aris could be my intellectual companion and sparring partner.

In contrast to Aris's world, the Greek world that I had known for the last four years seemed petty. I mean, tying strings to body parts, scaring pledges with threats of broken glass, locking people in homemade dungeons. What was the point of such antics? Passing time for a bunch of bored, rich kids. I suppose life with Liz would be similar: passing time, finding distractions to alleviate boredom, until my vitality gradually drained away.

By the time I reached Chicago, I was committed to doing my best in law school and to winning the big prize, a Supreme Court clerkship. That, of course, meant cozying up to Aris, however I felt about Chuck. It was time to quit being squeamish if I wanted to realize my dreams.

TWELVE

Back at school little had changed. The November 10 edition of the *Phoenix* read: "Kupow Affair Drags On." It was yet another piece critical of Miles. After I had finished the paper, I went to check my campus mailbox, where I found a note from Chuck requesting my presence that afternoon at the Four Seasons bar. I dreaded seeing him again, but thought that it could be a good opportunity to push him regarding Lee's readmission. Chuck had promised he could help me, and I felt strongly that I owed Lee.

At the appointed time, I found Chuck sitting in the darkest corner of the bar in a tall wing chair, his unusual looking head resting against one of the wings.

"Good evening," he said, motioning for me to take the other chair.

"What may I bring you?" asked an obsequious waiter right on my footsteps.

"Two Remy VSOPs," said Chuck before I could answer.

I settled into the other chair. "So when are you going to let Lee Gibbs onto the *Review*?" I came right out with it.

"I'm working on it," said Chuck, "but Miles is a problem."

"Have you seen Lee's article?"

"He's supposed to drop it off tonight."

"If Miles hasn't even read it, why is he being skeptical?"

"Miles thinks that even if Lee's piece is excellent, letting him on right now would be politically costly with this whole Kupow business. You know, another man and all."

"When are you going to put the whole Kupow thing to bed?"

"When Miles loses his position."

"Excuse me?" I asked, as the waiter delivered our drinks.

"Based on the criteria used to evaluate candidates for executive board positions, Miles was so far down the list that he probably wouldn't have even made book review editor."

"Really?" I leaned closer.

"The old chief, Henry Latham, had told me that I was going to be his replacement. Then, the week before the decision was announced, Judge Vanderlyden just happened to hire Latham's wife—who wasn't even on the *Review*—as a judicial clerk. It was a complete surprise to see Miles's name above mine."

"So, essentially, the chief's position should've been yours—and Aris, she should've had your job?"

"That's right. For all the lip service this country gives to equality of opportunity, things haven't changed all that much. Take someone like me, for example. I grew up on the south side, not far from the law school. My dad toiled away in the steel mill on the lake until it closed down. I had to work ten times as hard as Miles to even get admitted to this school. But no matter how hard I work, no matter how good I am, I still get pushed aside to make way for the Miles Vanderlydens of the world. It's about time for the tables to turn."

"But does it really matter who's number one versus number two?" I asked.

"Over the years, only about half of the junior editors on the executive board have received Supreme Court clerkships. The Court has never passed on an editor-in-chief."

"I didn't realize that."

Chuck smiled slyly. "Justice will be done my friend. For Mr. Gibbs. For Aris. For me."

He pulled two Monte Cristo cigars from his jacket, which we smoked with successive rounds of Remy. The drunker we became, the more viciously he complained of Miles's incompetence. Eventually, the substance of Chuck's complaints blended together, and I stopped listening. By nine, I was exhausted and told him that I had to be on my way.

Outside, it was drizzling, just enough to wet the streets. I walked along the busy sidewalk, admiring the glittering lights on Michigan Avenue and the glowing clouds as they wrapped around the towers. I felt nothing, and nothing felt good.

* * *

On Friday Chuck told me that Miles had rejected Lee's article. Miles had also recommended several days of arduous revisions before he would be willing to reconsider Lee's membership. Thus far, my unholy alliance with Chuck and Aris wasn't doing Lee much good.

When I arrived home around seven that evening, I had four messages on my machine, all from Lee, all equally despondent. In the last message, Lee explained that he had started drinking alone at the Metropolitan Club atop the Sears Tower and that he would appreciate some company. I decided to throw on a suit and join him.

It was already pretty cold, and the damp lake wind made it feel colder than the bank thermometers said it was, particularly as I walked across the exposed Monroe Street drawbridge. There was almost no one about. Even the homeless had withdrawn from the cold into the immense network of nineteenth-century tunnels beneath the city.

As I spun the revolving door and entered the lobby of the Sears Tower, a security guard approached me. "Can I help you, sir?"

"Yes, the Metropolitan Club."

"Take the third elevator bank to the sky bridge and follow the signs," he said, pointing to a hallway beyond a colorful modern statue.

"Thank you."

I walked along the rows and rows of elevators to the third bank, conveniently marked "Express to Sky Bridge."

When the elevator door opened, I was greeted by a hostess and led into a formal dining room.

I saw Lee leaning against a wall of glass with all of Chicago spread out beneath him.

"Sorry about the news," I said, joining him.

"Waiter." He waved his hand.

An elderly waiter hobbled over. "Yes, sir?"

"Another martini for me and the same for my friend."

"Yes, sir."

I glanced out the window next to me and realized that I was looking down on my own fifty-story apartment building.

"1500 feet," said Lee. "You might actually be able to say a prayer before you hit the ground."

Lee looked afire, reminding me of a painting that I had seen once at the Harper's Ferry Museum of the abolitionist John Brown—hair sticking up, cheeks red, eyes puffy, even a trickle of glistening mucus escaping his nostrils.

Lee wiped his nose with his napkin and sniffed.

"It's just a temporary delay," I said.

"Of my life."

The waiter deposited our drinks and hurried away.

"Be patient. Miles is just putting you in a holding pattern because of the Kupow affair."

"It doesn't really matter why. Miles screwed me in August and now he's screwing me again. Then because of the rules, now despite the rules."

"Just have another drink and calm down," I said.

Lee slammed the already empty martini glass on the table. "Oh, waiter."

The elderly waiter returned. "Yes, sir?"

"There's no one else at the bar, so I'd like to make a standing order on refills. You look over here and whenever you see that either my glass or my friend's glass is empty, we want another."

"Yes, sir. I will be right back, sir." The waiter looked scared.

"I know," said Lee. "It's all about saving Miles's ass, so he doesn't lose his precious little Supreme Court clerkship, so the faculty doesn't think that he's a misogynist."

"Chill," I said.

"You just don't understand how bad it's been. I worked my ass off last year—and then Miles decides that I should be booted. Because a mail room employee screws up. But the rules are the rules. So I play by their rules and work seventeen hours a day for six weeks, kissing Miles's ass, only to have him pull the rug out from under me and suspend the rules."

"You've done the work, just be patient. There's nothing you can do but keep playing their game."

"So you think there's nothing I can do?" he shouted, leaning across the table.

I shook my head in response to Lee's ranting.

"How about helping Miles to an untimely grave?" he whispered, squeezing his glass so hard I thought it would break.

"Come on," I said, looking into my drink, the liquid sloshing back and forth ever so slightly as the building swayed in the stiff Chicago wind.

"Almost every night I dream of killing him. Before you got here, I was thinking how Miles would look powerless, knowing he was about to die—"

"Lee," I said, raising both my open hands toward him to try to restore some sense of reason.

He leaned forward against my outstretched hands, speaking in a whisper. "I imagine that it's late at night and Miles is alone in his office. I walk right in and punch him in the face before he has a chance to say a word. He falls down. I pick up that trophy that's on his desk—you know, the one for graduating tops in his class at Andover—and smack him in the head. He's still looking up at me, but he's confused. Things up there," he pointed to my head, "just aren't working right anymore. But he knows that he's about to die. I smack him again, harder. It's just a matter of time until the bleeding inside his brain... ."

Lee sunk back into his chair. He was shaking violently.

I was afraid of him, and I was sure that he sensed it.

"Just joking," he said, laughing.

Lee went on and on like that. I was truly concerned that he might do something crazy, so I stayed with him until he passed out. I took him back to his place, and handed him off to the doorman, who promised to get him safely upstairs.

THIRTEEN

Aris and I had resumed our relationship, at least on platonic terms. We talked on the phone, had lunch, and went to movies. Though we weren't having sex, we were in many ways closer than we had ever been. So I was saddened to be taking her to the airport for Thanksgiving break.

"Why don't you come along?" she pleaded.

"You know better than anyone that I've got to work."

"I'm sorry. Dad and I will toast to you when we carve the turkey."

"Thanks."

"Gray?"

"Yes?"

"Could you ever love me again?"

I didn't know what to say. "What do you mean?"

"You used to say you loved me. You don't anymore, so I assumed—"

"I have a hard time trusting."

"Trusting me."

"It's not just you."

"I don't understand."

"Do you remember our first night, when you speculated about the women in those pictures, about why there were so many?"

"Yes."

"Each and every one of those women dumped me. Some passed me on after a couple of dates. Others strung me along for months. The last woman I dated before you, Melia—I caught her in my bed with two pledges. As Melia explained that night, I put the ladies to sleep."

"Oh, Gray," she said, touching my hand. "That's not true. It's not about that at all."

"What's it about then?"

"You've seen Chuck's dark side." She squeezed my hand.

"What's he holding over you?"

She squeezed even harder.

"You can't say, can you?"

"As much as I care about you, I've got to protect my dad. I'm all he has left. I just can't—"

"I understand."

She held my hand until we arrived at the United terminal. As she disappeared into the crowd of holiday travelers, my eyes filled with tears. I wished that I would have told her that I loved her—despite Chuck and his looming dark side.

I drove back to my apartment and settled into my growing backlog of work. I tried to not think about Aris and to instead focus on avoiding mediocrity. What I did now would determine whether I had an opportunity to make a difference, to be something more than a replaceable cog in the wheel of commerce. What does it matter, I thought, if some big firm lawyer dies at 40 or 60 instead of 80? At whatever point, someone else will step up to take his job, and do it adequately. In the end, it's unlikely that society will miss him. Most people are dispensable in this way. They're drones who will eventually be replaced by other drones. It was precisely such thinking that made me work from 5:30 in the morning until after midnight every night, outlining my courses and reading cases again and again.

On the Saturday before classes resumed, I was working late in my library cubicle when I was disturbed by Chuck's voice coming through the wall.

"Good to see you, sir," said Chuck.

"I wish I could say the same." I recognized Dean Simpson's voice.

"Oh."

"Was there something unclear about our conversation two weeks ago?"

"Excuse me?"

"I told you to readmit Kupow, did I not?"

"Sir, with all due respect, I believe that to do so would fundamentally undermine the *Review*."

"Son, forty-one years ago I held Miles's very position. Many good and bad leaders have come and gone since then, but the *Review* is still here. It's not the *Review*'s future that you should be worried about. It's your own."

"Excuse me, sir?"

"I understand what you're doing here so don't give me that bull about integrity that you don't have."

"Sir, with all due respect," urged Chuck.

"This is all about why you're not the chief."

"You know, then?" asked Chuck.

"What's happened can't be undone. Here, look at this—"

"What's this?" asked Chuck.

"Today's *New York Times*. On page three, there's a nasty article that paints the school in a poor light."

"Despite the injustice that I suffered, I would never do anything to compromise this school."

"Well, son, that's precisely what you and Ms. Byrd did—after I told you not to."

"It was not our—"

"I can assure you that neither Ms. Byrd nor you will ever have the opportunity to clerk for the Supreme Court. You will receive no recommendations from me or any other member of this faculty. Need I elaborate on what further harm can come to your careers if you continue to refuse my direction?"

"But sir—"

"Do you think for one minute that any member of this faculty would pin the blame for this mess on Miles Vanderlyden, son of the venerable Court of Appeals judge, grandson of the greatest New York trial attorney of the twentieth century? Miles Vanderlyden will get a Supreme Court clerkship with or without the faculty's help because of his family. So where does that leave a frustrated faculty? With you, son, and Ms. Byrd. It's your asses on the line here, not Vanderlyden's."

"But—"

"I don't have all evening. I take it that you now understand what needs to be done."

"I understand."

"I'll give you until next week. Good night then."

Seconds after the door shut, Chuck was on the phone. "May I speak with Aris?"

After a couple of minutes, Chuck continued. "Hey, baby. We've got big problems." Pause. "We can't talk on the phone. What flight are you on tomorrow?" Pause. "I'll be there. Bye."

When I got home that night, there was a message on my answering machine from Aris. She said that I didn't have to pick her up tomorrow because she was going to take a cab straight to the law school.

FOURTEEN

The next week, Aris had her hands full with the escalating *Law Review* mess, but she still made time for us. On Saturday she surprised me with tickets to the Children's Hospital Snow Ball, Chicago society's biggest Christmas party. She told me to meet her at the Chicago Cultural Center, 9:30 that night.

Upon arrival, I found a thousand people milling about in a huge ballroom. Black tailcoats with white ties, white evening gowns, black and white everywhere, only black and white. The dance floor and its orchestra took up the middle third of the ballroom. I didn't recognize the music, but it was brassy and swinging, reminiscent of the 1940's. Most of the twenty couples dancing looked quite accomplished, products of forced dance lessons in their youths. On both flanks of the dance floor rows and rows of tables went off as far as I could see. Each table buzzed with activity, a mini-swarm of beautiful young Chicagoans surrounding a centerpiece ice carving of a snowman. Then I looked up into the domed ceiling. Gold leaf and blue mosaic patterns, the names of classical writers circling the dome. Plato, Homer, Virgil, Horace.

I made my way to a bar at the edge of the dance floor and picked up an Absolut Citron martini, generously poured. I sipped away while scanning the tables along the dance floor in search of Aris. When I finished my drink, I returned to the bar for another and then resumed my search. Every thin woman with dark hair resembled Aris, and faces were blurring amid the dizzying contrast of black and white.

When I reached the end of the left flank of tables without any luck, I turned around and headed in the opposite direction, across the dance floor. Above the fray, I noticed a woman perched on a window ledge, about five feet up. It was Aris, of course, gazing out over the crowd, her back against the wide marble window frame, her long legs stretching horizontally along the sill, cocooned in a white sequined gown. Yet as I moved closer, she looked burdened. I stopped walking and simply stared. I watched her eyes. They were blank, without focus or movement.

I started toward her again, walking to within three feet of her window before she noticed me.

"Hi," she said.

"How did you manage to get up there?"

"Chuck gave me a boost."

Before I could ask why, she said, "There were no more chairs. Chuck grabbed the last one."

Her eyes turned toward my left, and sure enough, there was Chuck. His white hair matched his tie.

"Just you two?"

"No, Miles and Katie are at the bar with some Andover people. They've invited us to an after-party over on the Gold Coast."

"Whose party?"

"Miles's ex-girlfriend, Susan."

"That sounds interesting."

"Did you hear already?" she asked.

"Hear what?"

"Judge Vanderlyden received a mail bomb today."

"Is he okay?"

"The marshals x-ray all of his mail. They found it in time."

"No wonder you're despondent."

"Gray, dear, let's dance." Aris swung her legs off the window sill. I helped her down, and she wrapped her arms around me, giving me a long, soft kiss.

"Now that's better," I said.

When we reached the dance floor, I stopped her and watched the fast-moving couples spin by.

"I'm not a sophisticated dancer," I confessed.

"That's fine. I'm not in the mood for fancy stuff."

I placed both my hands around Aris's lower back and led her to the center of the dance floor, barely escaping the acrobats whirling around the periphery.

For the first time since I had known Aris, she seemed stiff.

We danced to the next dozen songs. By the time we took a break for water, Aris was smiling, but she was still not herself.

We started back to her table. As we approached, I could see Chuck still sitting there. His eyes were on us, following our every move.

"There's Miles," said Aris, diverting us away from Chuck.

"Hu—llo!" Miles slurred, shaking my hand. He kept pumping it up and down and up and down.

"Hello again," I said, pulling free.

A very pretty blonde came up behind Miles and rested her chin on his shoulder. "Who's this?" she asked.

"It's... it's—" said Miles.

"Grayson Bullock," I said, extending my hand.

"Susan Morrison," she replied, holding my hand and then sliding around Miles to kiss my cheek. As she backed away, my eyes were drawn to her ample cleavage.

I felt Aris put her arm around me.

"Nice to meet you," I said, noticing that Susan's hand was now resting on Miles's hip.

"It's 11:30," said Susan. "I say we start making our way to my place and avoid the wicked cloak line."

"Where's Katie?" asked Aris.

Miles rolled his eyes.

"We can't leave without Katie," said Aris, looking around. "I'll go find her." Aris walked off toward their table.

Miles and Susan leaned closer. "We used to be in love," he whispered.

"Quit it," said Susan. She teasingly slapped his chest with her free hand.

I could see Aris, Katie, and Chuck approaching through the crowd.

"Here comes Katie," I warned. Susan disengaged Miles and put her arm around me. I felt her lips against my ear. "Even when he's drunk, he's still such the dashing figure," she whispered.

The other three joined us.

"Ready?" asked Aris.

Katie was all red and blotchy, and she looked as if she had been crying.

"Chip," shouted Susan toward the bar.

A tall, effeminate man with dusty blond hair turned. "Yeeeesss, dear?" he replied, lifting a wine glass in our direction, a ringed-pinkie outstretched.

"After party."

"Yes, let's."

"What was your name again?" asked Susan, putting her arm in mine.

"Grayson Bullock."

"Grayson, this is Chip Endicott." We shook hands.

"A pleasure," said Chip, taking my other arm.

"Nice to meet you," I said.

Susan and Chip escorted me, arm-in-arm, to the cloak room, as if we had known each other all of our lives. It was awkward, but I appreciated being the center of attention.

After retrieving our coats, we wandered outside en masse. It was really cold, probably fifteen degrees. I put on my gloves and waved for a cab, but the wind cut right through, and my fingers started to get numb. We eventually managed to get two cabs. The others took the lead cab while Chuck, Aris, and I took the second.

"Follow that cab," I instructed, having no idea where Susan lived.

I took off my gloves and rubbed my hands trying to warm them.

"What's wrong?" asked Aris.

"My hands," I said.

"Let me see those gloves," said Chuck, grabbing one from my lap.

Chuck felt inside and started to laugh. "These are crap. You need to go down to Burberry's and get some with cashmere lining."

He tossed the glove back into my lap.

I heard cars honking as the cab ran the busy red light at Michigan and Ohio to stay behind Miles's cab.

"Everything okay up there?" I asked the cabby.

He shrugged. Despite the close call, we managed to pull into Susan's building just behind the others.

Everyone piled out, greeted the doorman, and boarded an

ornate brass elevator with keyholes for every floor except the lobby. Susan turned her key, and we ascended to the sixth floor. When the elevator door opened, there was a small foyer—a mirror, a painting of a bowl of fruit, and a hall tree for coats. Susan tossed her overcoat on the hall tree, and we all did the same before following her into a sitting room filled with antiques.

"This is the art room," said Susan, pointing to two paintings on opposite walls: "Courbet and Corot."

"Please, everyone have a seat," said Chip. "We'll be back shortly with some champagne."

After Chip and Susan left, we took positions on the two long blue couches and the two tall golden armchairs that were arranged opposite one another around a floral needlepoint rug.

Aris and I had chosen one of the couches, Katie and Miles the other, and Chuck had flopped himself into one of the giant armchairs.

"I suppose a crown is in order," Chuck said, patting his hair down.

"It would be a tight fit," said Aris.

"Now, now," said Chuck.

"Champagne is served," said Susan, returning with seven empty Waterford flutes. Chip was in immediate tow, lugging a giant silver bucket with three bottles of Salon.

Susan handed a glass to everyone while Chip set the ice bucket in a stand next to the couch. He pulled out a bottle with a big "S" on its side. POP!

Chip circled the room, pouring everyone's glass half full.

When Chip had finally filled his own, Susan lifted her glass in Miles's direction. "Cheers." Before we had finished toasting, Susan joined Miles on the other couch, actually sitting between Katie and him.

"So you're all law students?" asked Susan, looking back and forth between Chuck, Aris, and me.

"Yes," said Aris, "and you're—"

"I help manage my family's portfolio."

"I work for the fund, too," said Chip, who had settled into the other armchair. "A lot of flying to obscure corners of the world."

"We'd still be in the rain forest if poor Chip had avoided taking a dip in the Amazon."

"I was treading water when I saw this giant water beetle—the size of my thumb—dive right down into my shorts," he said, pointing below his waist.

"And it bit him right on the," said Susan, pointing to her groin.

"We understand," said Aris.

"By the time we got back to our hotel room, the bitten area had become extremely swollen," said Chip.

"Are you well now?" asked Katie.

"I'm still sore, but the doctor expects a quick recovery."

I finished the last of my champagne.

"More Salon?" asked Chip, pulling another bottle from the bucket. POP!

He went around the room, refilling everyone's glasses.

"Would anyone like something to eat?" asked Susan, touching Miles's thigh.

"Sure," replied Miles, "I'm famished."

No one else expressed interest one way or another.

"We're going to the kitchen to see what we can forage up," said Susan, literally pulling Miles from the couch.

Katie looked disgusted.

No sooner did they leave the room than did Chip let out a squeal. "Excuse me," said Chip, hurrying off through another doorway.

"What do you suppose is wrong with him?" asked Aris.

"He just can't hold his liquor," said Chuck.

"Egad! Ah!" We heard Chip scream.

"Perhaps this has something to do with a giant water beetle," I said.

Chip, shirt untucked, zipper still half way down, returned to the living room. "Please tell Susan that I have evacuated myself to Northwestern Hospital's emergency care."

He sprinted out the front door.

"I hope he's okay," said Aris.

"He's probably just hatched a litter of Amazonian water beetles," said Chuck.

"Shouldn't we tell Susan?" asked Aris.

"Yes, I think we should find her this instant," said Katie.

"Let's do," said Chuck, standing. "Dey went dat-a-way."

"Yes," said Katie, "get going." She gave Chuck a shove, making him spill champagne all over his shirt.

"A wabbit hunting we will go," said Chuck, tiptoeing slowly.

Katie walked briskly around him, and we followed.

We went through an unlit library and the dining room before reaching the kitchen. There was no sign of anyone. Nor was there any sign of any attempt at food preparation.

"Hmmmm," said Chuck, "bery, bery suspicious."

"Miles was really drunk," added Aris.

Katie now looked panicked.

We heard something above us that sounded like Susan's voice.

"Was that her?" asked Katie.

"Sounded like her," I said.

"What did she say?" asked Katie.

"It wasn't a say," said Chuck. "It was more of a moan."

Katie burst through the opposite doorway to find a plush family room with a giant television and spiral staircase leading upstairs, but there was no sign of Miles or Susan.

The rhythmic whimpering was louder though, coming from upstairs.

"Surely not," I said.

Katie silently climbed the spiral staircase, and we followed.

On the second floor, we found ourselves in a dark hallway. The sounds, clearly of a sexual nature, were coming from the closest door, the only one emitting any light.

Katie threw open the door with a thump—and immediately fainted. I caught her before she could hit the floor. By the time I finally managed to look inside, Miles was sitting on the floor trying to put himself back inside his pants. A gloating Susan was sitting on the bed topless. She was smiling.

"What are you doing barging into my bedroom?" asked Susan, trying to sound upset, but then she started to laugh. "I'm sorry," she said, covering her mouth.

"Chip has gone to the emergency room at Northwestern," said Chuck.

"Is it the bite?" she asked.

"We believe so."

"Look," said Susan, "just make yourselves comfortable. I'll be back later."

Susan forced her way by us and conveniently fled down the stairway.

"Wow," I said, still holding the unconscious Katie.

By now, Miles had his zipper up, but he still looked rather confused.

"Put her on the bed," said Aris.

"Chuck, give me a hand here," I said.

Chuck and I managed to hoist Katie onto the bed.

"If you could just leave her alone with me," Miles said. He stood up, but was so drunk that he had to grab the bedpost for support.

"After she comes to," said Aris.

Miles leaned toward Katie.

"Give her some space," said Aris.

Miles refused to back away, but Katie was already coming to.

No sooner did Katie's eyes focus on Miles than she attacked him, slapping his face again and again. "Aaaaaa, eeeee!" she screamed.

I jumped on top of Katie, pinning both her arms to the bed and sitting atop her chest. This gave Chuck enough time to pull Miles out of range of Katie's flailing feet.

She used all of her strength trying to break my hold, even bouncing her body up and down on the bed.

"Calm down! Calm down!" I shouted.

Katie's squirming stopped and turned into tears.

She was now babbling, "You promised. No other women. Just me. We were going to get married. If I'd move to Chicago, you'd marry me." Anyway, it was something like that, over and over again, until she just sat there, stuffed up, all red and puffy, and sniffling.

All the while, Miles, from a safe distance, was drunkenly proclaiming his sorrow and begging her forgiveness.

I climbed off of Katie carefully, and she just lay there, staring at the ceiling.

Miles clambered to her side and started whispering in her ear. He held her left hand in his and started to stroke her hair.

Katie pulled her hand free, sat up, slapped Miles in the face, and walked right by us without a word.

Miles crawled into a corner and started to cry.

"I think you need a few moments to reflect," said Aris, as she turned off the lights.

"Time to go," she whispered, pulling Chuck and me outside and closing the door.

We returned to the kitchen and raided the fridge. Aris and I had turkey sandwiches while Chuck took a pile of caviar into the family room and powered up the sixty-inch TV.

Within minutes, we could hear him snoring.

Aris and I decided to take a tour of the house, which went on and on, encompassing two whole floors of a high-rise that had to itself encompass at least one-third of a city block. Downstairs, there were no bedrooms, only strings of formal rooms and the more casual home theater.

We went back upstairs, passed the ignominious room where Miles was now silent, and tried door after door before finally finding the master bedroom, which was situated on the corner of the building. Two walls of glass looked out over the partially frozen lake.

We walked over to the giant sleigh bed, undressed, and embraced. As we began to make love, I looked past Aris at the mosaic of ice flowing across the black lake. The reunion of our bodies was awkward at first and not as special as it had been. I was distracted by the thought of having to share her. Yet as the night went on, those concerns gradually receded. When we tenderly shuddered, I found myself wanting to whisper, "I love you." It seemed such an indecorous use of the words.

Aris rested in my arms for a while. I could tell she was still awake because every time she blinked her eyes, her eyelashes tickled my chest.

Eventually, I could feel my arm falling asleep so I shifted, forcing her to sit up.

"The haze of love," I mumbled as I stretched.

Aris placed her slender finger on my lips. "Our imaginations are free from reality," she whispered.

After Aris fell asleep, I lay awake thinking about her words. My imagination was hardly free from the sex that she shared with Chuck and my own self-contempt for letting Chuck have his way. That's the problem with being with someone who is unable or unwilling to give herself completely to you. It's the realization that you're just not good enough, not special enough to receive exclusivity. This awareness, that the person you love is also leading a life with someone else, is about as dark a feeling as a human being can experience.

FIFTEEN

The next morning I went back to Presidential Towers by myself. No matter how hard I tried to study, my mind kept returning to Aris and our struggling love. Even if we both loved each other, the survival of our relationship depended upon the fiction that we did not. Aris possessed the seed of a conscience and so did I. To acknowledge love would demand exclusivity. Aris certainly wasn't willing to pay the professional price of that exclusivity, and I wasn't entirely sure that I was either.

Later that evening, I drove down to the law school, hoping to find Aris. I ended up running into Miles just outside of the *Law Review* offices.

"Oh, hi," I said.

Miles blushed. "I must apologize for my behavior."

"I've seen worse," I said, trying to make him feel better.

"I was utterly drunk and worried. Do you even know about the bomb?"

"Aris told me."

"Speaking of Aris, is she here yet?"

"No. Is she supposed to be?"

"Chuck's called a meeting for 9:30."

"Oh." I looked at my watch. It was only 7:30.

"Please excuse me," said Miles. He walked over to the *Law Review* office, unlocked its door, and went inside.

I settled into my cubicle and started reading the next week's assignments. I had studied for some time before I realized that it was snowing outside, as hard as I had ever seen it snow. Giant, fluffy, round flakes, some as big as my fist, tumbled against the window, making audible splats. I stopped, in awe of the spectacle, and watched as the snow piled up on top of the little lamps that illuminated the dark courtyard below.

I checked my watch—9:25—and thought of Aris.

I decided to loiter outside the Green Lounge to see whether I could intercept her before the meeting.

On my way down the library stairwell, I met Lee.

"Hey," I said.

Lee looked pale and sickly.

"You're usually not here so late," he said.

"I went to this party last night so I'm trying to catch up. Are you feeling okay?" I asked, touching his cold arm.

"I've been sleeping here all week, trying to finish their edits."

"They let you stay here overnight?"

The half-dozen books that he was holding spilled, bouncing down the stairwell.

"You really need to take a day off and get some sleep," I said, helping him retrieve the books.

"I will, as soon as I finish."

"The revisions?"

"Yeah, the damn revisions," he snapped. He grabbed the books I had gathered and headed upstairs.

I walked down to the Green Lounge, waited until 9:35 and then concluded that Aris had probably gone up in the elevator while I was detained by Lee.

I returned to my cubicle. Sure enough, I heard Aris's voice through the wall.

"... softheartedness," she said.

"We can scream at each other all night if you wish, but I'm not changing my mind. Mary's back on as of tomorrow."

"I know you feel guilty about last night," said Chuck.

"What!"

"Your fiancée catching you with another woman and all, particularly one who's so much prettier."

"Leave my personal life out of this," said Miles.

"Why?" asked Chuck. "Your judgment is at issue, and your behavior last night reflected incredibly poor judgment."

"This is a letter announcing your resignation," said Aris. "If you refuse to sign it—"

"What? You're going to tell the whole world about Susan?"

"That's not necessary if—" said Aris.

"I'll deny it. So will Susan and Katie."

"We have a videotape," said Aris.

"See for yourself," said Chuck.

After a pause, I could hear last night's moaning, accentuated by Miles's chants of "Oh, Susan. Milk me baby."

I cringed.

"Later on," said Chuck, "you're so drunk you can't stand up, then you cry like a baby, and as an encore, you projectile vomit."

"This law school doesn't care about my personal life, and Katie already knows."

"But do Katie's parents know?" asked Aris.

"You little bitch."

"And what if copies start showing up in the justices' chambers?" asked Chuck.

"I'll see you both in court for this. Blackmailers—you don't know who you're dealing with. You may humiliate me, but I'll destroy you! Long after people have forgotten about this tape, Chuck, you'll be processing welfare claims for your lousy white trash relatives."

"Gray," I heard Lee say from behind.

I jumped and turned. "What's up?"

"I'm sorry about earlier. It's just hard to keep a cheery disposition in the face of all this."

"I understand. Really, I do," I said, trying to listen to what was happening in the *Review* office. All I could hear was shifting, like chairs moving.

"You were trying to be helpful earlier, and I'm sorry," said Lee.

"Hey, no big deal. I'd already forgotten about it. But look, I've got to meet Aris," I said, glancing at my watch.

"I see," said Lee.

When he turned to walk away, he slammed into the next table.

"Are you all right?"

"Yeah, yeah," said Lee, "everything will turn around soon." He held his hip as he hobbled away.

I gathered up my books, tossed them into my backpack, and walked over to the elevator foyer outside the *Review* office.

Seeing the office door was still closed, I waited. After a few minutes, I ducked into the restroom.

Chuck walked in as I was standing at the urinal.

"Oh, hello," I said.

He jumped.

I noticed that he was wearing his big, leather, wool-cuffed coat, apparently on his way out.

"Aris hasn't left yet, has she?" I asked.

"About to. It looks like there's a lot of snow, so we're going to walk back rather than drive."

"Why don't you let me give you a ride in my four by four," I said, zipping up my pants.

"That'll be fine," said Chuck, moving toward the urinal.

I left Chuck alone in the restroom and returned to the foyer.

Aris was standing in front of the *Law Review*'s open doorway, looking distraught.

"Hi," I said.

She jumped. "Oh, hi," she said, holding her hand over her chest.

"Chuck said you two need a ride because of the snow."

"Sure."

"What about Miles?" I asked.

"He's already left."

"Why don't you grab your coat?"

"Chuck and I have to talk about some *Law Review* business first. It'll take about fifteen minutes."

"But Chuck's already wearing his coat."

"He's not leaving until we've had a chance to talk."

"Mind if I wait inside?" I asked.

"Where's your truck?"

"In the parking lot."

"Why don't you bring it around and warm it up?"

"Sure. See you in fifteen minutes."

I headed downstairs.

The security guard stopped me on my way out. "Let me check your bag."

I opened my backpack, and he glanced quickly through my books. "Okay," he said.

I put on my gloves and headed outside into about five inches of snow. It was still falling as fast as it had been earlier. I started my Explorer and pulled it up to the front of the parking lot, as close as possible to the exit doors. Realizing that I was just below the *Law Review*'s third-floor offices, I gazed up, trying to make out Aris and Chuck through the blowing snow.

While I was looking up, waiting for the lights to go out, I heard a knock at my passenger window and turned to see Aris. I unlocked the doors, and she climbed in, leaning across to give me a peck on the lips.

"Is Chuck coming?" I asked.

"He ran out to his car to get some books that he'd left in the trunk."

I heard the rear door behind my seat open and felt a cold blast of snow.

"Thanks a lot for the ride," said Chuck, closing the door and patting my shoulder.

"You left the lights on," I said, pointing to their offices.

"Miles is still working," said Chuck.

"He came back right after you left," said Aris quickly, "after he saw how deep the snow was. We offered him your ride, but he wanted to get some letters out."

I turned up the heater and pulled away, easily gliding through the snow.

With the exception of the snow emergency route that ran along the Midway, Hyde Park was unplowed and, for the most part, free of other vehicles. Aris's Saab would have never made it.

"This will do," said Chuck, as I slowed in front of their building.

Chuck patted me on the shoulder and hopped out into the snow, before I had even come to a complete stop.

I watched Chuck in my side mirror as he went up the building's steps and disappeared inside.

"Your place," said Aris, patting my thigh.

Once back at Presidential Towers, we had quick, tired sex, then I fell asleep.

SIXTEEN

The *"buzz, buzz, buzz"* of my alarm clock woke us just before six. By 6:30 we were out the door and by just after seven had pulled into the unplowed parking lot at the law school.

"A foot," I said.

"Eight inches," said Aris.

"It looks like a lot to me."

We were the first car to arrive that morning, though twenty or so snow-covered vehicles littered the lot.

"The library's still closed, but you can study in my office."

"Great," I said, relishing my first opportunity to work on hallowed ground.

Aris called the elevator and used a key to dispatch it to the *Law Review* foyer on the third floor. She used another key to unlock the *Law Review* office door.

The moment the door opened, I was greeted by a blast of freezing cold air. "Turn on some heat," I said.

Aris walked over and turned up the thermostat.

"Miles turned off the heat yet forgot to switch off the lights," I observed.

"The heat automatically turns off," said Aris.

"Where should I work?" I asked.

"Why don't you set yourself up in my office, the last room through that door." She pointed to my left.

I opened the first door and passed into a long rectangular room filled with computers, and then tried to open the next door, but it was partially jammed. I stuck my head through the gap to see someone face-down, prone on the floor. I forced my way through the narrow gap. It was Miles.

My first thought was that he had decided to sleep on the floor because of the blizzard.

I knelt down. "Miles. Hey, Miles, are you all right?"

I touched his neck. Cold. Hard. No pulse.

I placed my hand against his mouth. No breath.

I felt something damp on my hand. I looked down to see my hand covered with a sticky black syrup.

"He's killed himself," I mumbled.

At that moment, Aris came through the door so quickly that the door knocked me over and onto Miles's body. Before I could get back up, Aris started screaming. She pushed me aside and rolled Miles over. I grabbed Aris and tried to pull her away from the body, but she wouldn't release him. I ended up pulling them both halfway across the room.

Aris, seemingly in shock, cradled Miles's bloody head in her lap while I called 911.

"Please describe your emergency."

"There's a man injured, bleeding from his head. I think it's a gunshot wound."

"Where are you?"

"University of Chicago Law School Library, third floor, *Law Review* office."

"I'm dispatching now," she said.

I hung up just as Chuck walked in.

"Is he?" asked Chuck, a little too calmly.

I nodded, but Aris's eyes were still glazed over. She kept rubbing Miles's matted hair as if she were petting a dog.

"You hold her," said Chuck. "I'll put him back."

I grabbed Aris's sticky hands and pulled them away while Chuck dragged Miles's body back by the pool of blood.

My eye caught a book on the floor next to Miles. The spine was facing upward, its pages fanning out and crushed against the floor. A blue constitutional law book by someone named Gunther. I noticed that some of the little gold letters along the spine were stained. Others were rubbed off. I leaned in closer. The stain looked like blood. In the dried blood, there were pieces of dark hair, like Miles's.

"Look at this," I said.

Aris continued to sit on the floor, staring into space, but Chuck walked over and knelt beside me.

I heard doors slamming outside and stood up. Down below, in the snow-covered parking lot, I could see three university police cars and an ambulance.

I looked back down at the book. "Maybe it wasn't a gunshot wound."

Chuck nodded.

"Aris," I said, waving my hand in front of her face. There was no response.

Two paramedics and two police officers burst into the room. I grabbed Aris and guided her to the far side of the room, away from the body.

One of the paramedics rolled Miles over and felt for a pulse.

He opened one of Miles's eyelids, then he shook his head.

"He's been dead for some time," said the paramedic.

"Looks like a gunshot," said one of the police officers pointing at the pool of blood on the floor.

"Come look at this book," I said.

The officers looked around at the hundreds of books lining the walls. One asked, "Which book?"

"The big blue one—there on the floor." I pointed.

The officers gathered around the book.

"Yep," one said.

"Let's go," said another officer, grabbing me by the arm.

"You, too, lady," he said, pulling Aris as well.

"Let go of me," she said and twisted herself free.

We walked out to the elevator foyer. Chuck was already there, speaking with a group of other officers. They questioned us perfunctorily about how we had come to find the body. Then Dean Simpson came upon our group. Looking flustered, he kept asking, "What's happened here? What's happened here?"

"Miles is dead," said Aris, holding up her bloody hands.

"What?" asked Dean Simpson, his voice trailing off.

"It looks like foul play," said an officer.

"Do you need these three?" asked Simpson.

"Na. The victim's been dead for hours. They just found the body."

"Come with me," said Simpson.

We walked across the library to the faculty elevator,

descended to the first floor hallway, and then followed the dean past the receptionist desk to a large office overlooking the courtyard and the fountain.

"What on Earth happened?" he asked, closing the door.

"We don't know," said Chuck.

"He was just there," I said.

Dean Simpson paged through a Rolodex and then picked up the phone, dialing frantically.

"This is Dean Simpson from Chicago."

Pause.

"Sure."

He covered the receiver and spoke toward us, "Wait in the hall."

We went outside and closed the door.

About ten minutes later, Dean Simpson opened the door and invited us back in.

"What's your name?" he asked in my direction.

"Grayson Bullock, sir."

"Are you a one L?"

"Yes, sir."

"Listen, the FBI is sending a team here from downtown."

We nodded.

"I'm going to tell the university police to wait for the FBI. If I don't, they're liable to destroy evidence."

Dean Simpson left us. We sat there silently staring out at the gardeners as they cleared snow from the courtyard.

"Do you think it was related to the threats?" I finally asked.

"It seems more likely that it was random crime, don't you think?" asked Chuck.

"But they just sent a bomb to Judge Vanderlyden—and then this?"

Aris stared outside, obviously distraught. "The snow is very pretty."

"Didn't you lock the door on your way out?" I asked in Chuck's direction.

"No. The last person out locks the door. Miles was the last one there, fortunately for me."

"So anyone could've walked in there while Miles was working?"

"I suppose so."

"But wasn't it locked this morning?" I asked in Aris's direction, remembering her keys.

"I think it's going to be a wet winter," she said.

"Maybe we should take her over to the hospital," I said.

Aris's eyes returned to life. "Congratulations," she said, looking toward Chuck. "You're editor-in-chief."

Chuck almost smiled, but his jaw quickly stiffened.

"So why not the South Americans?" I asked again.

"They would've shot him execution-style to send a message to the judiciary," said Chuck, pointing to the back of his head.

"Why are you so sure he wasn't shot?" asked Aris.

Neither of us answered.

"What about your friend Lee?" asked Chuck.

"What?"

"Or Katie," said Aris. "They could've had a fight of some kind after we left."

"She often came to the offices when Miles was working late," said Chuck.

I remembered how it took all of my strength to pin her down on the bed Saturday night.

"Of course, we mustn't rule out Mary Kupow or one of the nuts who chased Miles halfway across the city," I offered.

Dean Simpson returned with two FBI agents, and we shut up.

"These are Agents Zero and Maxwell from the Chicago office."

They weren't much older than us, wearing navy suits with white shirts and red-patterned ties.

"Which were the two who first found the body?" asked Agent Zero.

"The lady and this man," said Dean Simpson, pointing at me.

"I'll take the lady," said Agent Maxwell.

"You're with me then," said Zero.

As Aris and I followed the agents outside, I could hear Dean

Simpson's words trailing off: "We can't let this tragedy interfere with our publishing deadlines… ."

Agent Zero led me into a back administrative office down the hall. I turned just as Aris gave me a hard look.

Zero sat down first. I waited for a moment, staring down at his bald spot and thinking about how his buzz haircut made it less noticeable.

"Sit there," said Zero, pointing to a second chair.

I did as he directed.

"I don't suppose you'll be needing an attorney for this talk?" asked Zero, clicking a pen.

"No, sir. I wish to help you in any way possible."

"Well, that's the kind of response we dream about. But then, you're not a suspect, are you?"

I tried to smile.

"I want you to walk me through this morning, the events just before you found the body," said Zero.

"Aris and I drove in—"

"From where?"

"My apartment."

"She picked you up this morning?"

"She spent the night."

"Where is this apartment of yours?"

"Downtown."

"You're romantically involved?"

"Yes."

"How did she get to your apartment?"

"I drove her—because of the snow."

I watched Zero scribble, awaiting his next question.

"Just go on with your story whenever I stop talking."

"We arrived at the law school just after seven."

"Were you the only car in the parking lot?"

"No. There were several others, but they were all covered with snow."

"Do you remember seeing tire tracks in the snow?" he asked.

"Mine were the first."

"Go on."

"We parked in the lot out back and entered by the security desk. The door was open, but no one was around. We took the elevator from the first floor to the third floor. We got off in the foyer, and went into the *Law Review* office."

"Why did you go there?"

"It's Aris's office. That's where she studies in the morning before class."

"Did you often study in her office?"

"This was the first time."

"Why did you go there today then?"

"Because I drove her in. Because of the snow."

"Okay," said Zero, clicking his pen.

"I went to set up my books in the back office, but the door wouldn't open all the way."

"What do you mean 'the door wouldn't open all of the way?'"

"I pushed, but could only open it this much," I said, holding my hands up to show the distance of about a foot.

"So what did you do then?"

"I stuck my head through to see what was blocking the door."

"That's when you saw Miles?"

I nodded.

"Describe his position."

"He was face down, his head against the door … the rest of his body was perpendicular to the door."

"Did you move him then?"

"When I squeezed through the doorway, I think I moved him a little bit."

"Did you touch him?"

"I called to him first. I thought he might have slept on the floor with the storm and all."

"But then you touched him?"

"I touched his neck for a pulse."

"Why did you do that?"

"To see whether he was alive."

"Did he look dead?"

"I'd never seen a dead person before."

"When you touched him, how did he feel?"

"Cold, really cold."

"And was there a pulse?"

"No. No." I shook my head.

"Was that the only time you touched the body?"

"No. I went to feel for his breath and got my hands in this cold goop on the floor. When I raised my hand, I saw it covered with blood."

"Bright red blood?" he asked, holding up his red pen.

"No, dark, almost black, I think."

"Did you call the police then?"

"No. Right then Aris came in and knocked me over with the door. By the time I came to my feet, Aris was screaming and cradling Miles's head. I tried to pull her away, but I ended up dragging them across the room."

"So you slid the body across the room?" He looked exasperated.

"I didn't mean to," I said, looking down at the now-dried blood on my hand.

"When did you call the police?"

"Then."

"So Aris sat there holding the body while you called?"

"Yeah."

"How did the body get moved back to the door?"

"Chuck arrived, and he helped me separate Aris from the body. He pulled Miles's body back by the puddle of blood."

"The same place where you found it?"

"Not exactly."

"Did you touch the book?"

"No."

"Did any of the others touch the book?"

"No."

"At least we have one untainted piece of evidence," he said, clicking his pen twice.

"Did you know the victim?" asked Zero.

"Yes."

"How long?"

"A couple of months."

"How did you meet him?"

"Through Aris. We had enjoyed his company on a number of social occasions, including a visit by his father, Judge Vanderlyden."

"When was the last time that you saw him?"

"Last night."

"What time?"

"Around 7:30."

"What was he doing? Studying?"

"*Law Review* work. He was an editor, like Aris."

"What's *Law Review*?"

"It's sort of a legal magazine," I said, passing him an issue from a nearby shelf.

He paged through the journal and put it down.

"What happened next?"

"Aris, Chuck, and Miles had a *Law Review* meeting."

"Did you witness any of this meeting?"

I started to sweat and could feel my heart accelerating. "No," I lied.

"When was the meeting over?"

"Around ten."

"How do you know that?"

"I was waiting for Aris outside the office, by the elevator."

"Who did you see then?"

"Chuck and Aris."

"What about Miles?"

"Oh yeah," I said. I lied again, remembering the discrepancy between Aris saying that Miles had already left and then Chuck saying that he was back in the office.

"I thought you said that you last saw him at 7:30?"

"I mean that I heard him talking in the office."

Zero narrowed his eyes and pursed his lips. "So after the meeting was adjourned, what happened?"

"Miles stayed behind to work. I gave Chuck a ride to his apartment. Aris came home with me."

"What do you mean, 'came home'?" asked Zero, clicking his pen quickly.

"Like I already said, she spent the night."

The clicking continued.

"She spent the entire night with you?"

"Yes."

"Were Aris, Chuck, and Miles on good terms?"

"The best," I lied.

"Can you think of anything else strange that happened recently?"

"You know about the bomb."

He stopped clicking. "Yes. Anything else?"

"Some liberal students hated Miles. They once chased him and pelted him with eggs."

"I don't know about that."

"He was hated by some students for having expelled a young woman, Mary Kupow, from *Law Review* earlier this fall."

"Anything else?"

I thought about Katie and the events of the Ball. "Saturday night, Miles's fiancée caught him in bed with another woman."

"The night before he was killed?"

I nodded.

"Now that's interesting." He smiled, clicking his pen rapidly. "How do you know about this?"

"I was at the party where it happened."

"What does that mean?"

"A group of us, including Katie, barged in on Miles when he was having intercourse with another woman."

"Who was this other woman?"

"Susan. I don't recall her last name."

"Is that all?" he asked.

"Yes, sir."

"Go find your friend, Mr. Hellar, and send him in."

"Sure," I said, heading back toward Dean Simpson's office. The door was closed so I knocked.

"Come in," said Dean Simpson.

I did. Chuck was still sitting there, but Aris was nowhere to be seen.

"Chuck, the agent would like to talk to you," I said.

Chuck glared at me as if I were responsible for Agent Zero's interest.

"Where is he?"

"Third door on the right."

"Now Chuck," said Dean Simpson, "get those letters out today."

"But sir, I need to have access to my office."

"I'll get you the letterhead, and you can use my computer."

"Yes, sir," said Chuck. He walked by me with a scowl.

Before I could take my seat, Aris returned with Agent Maxwell.

"Mind if I talk with you for a moment, Mr. Bullock?" asked Maxwell.

"No," I said. I followed the agent down the same hall. Walking behind him, I stared at the wrinkled mess of his suit jacket and wondered how long it had been since it had visited a cleaners. He escorted me into another small administrative room, and we sat down.

"How long have you known Lee Gibbs?"

I was surprised at his interest in Lee. "Going on five years. He was a year ahead of me in my fraternity at the University of Texas."

"Did you see Gibbs last night?"

"A few times."

"How did he look?"

"Tired."

"Why did you think that he was tired?"

"He just looked tired."

"Did Gibbs and the victim get along?"

"To the best of my knowledge, yes."

"Did Gibbs like the victim?"

"Their interactions were strictly professional."

"Did Gibbs ever threaten the victim?"

"No."

"Didn't you tell Ms. Byrd that Gibbs had spoken of killing the victim?"

"I vaguely remember him saying something along those lines—"

"What did Gibbs tell you?"

"I can't remember exactly."

"Did he threaten to kill Vanderlyden?"

"No."

"Did he speak of how he wanted to kill Vanderlyden."

"Let me try to remember." I sat there for a few minutes, trying to recall the night at the Metropolitan Club. "I'm afraid that I'll misstate what Lee said."

"Let me try to refresh your memory. Byrd said that Gibbs had told you about an elaborate plan to murder the victim, the conclusion of which involved the smashing in of the victim's head with a blunt object, precisely what appears to have occurred here." He glared at me in obvious frustration.

"All I can remember is that he had a bad dream with Miles in it," I lied.

"The conclusion of this dream was Vanderlyden's death?"

"Yes," I said.

"Why didn't you say so the first time that I asked you?"

"I didn't want to mislead you."

"But you did when you said that you couldn't remember, when, in fact, you could."

"I'm sorry," I said, twisting my sweaty hands.

"When did you last see Gibbs?" asked Maxwell.

"Around ten, just before I met Aris and Chuck."

"So he was in the library when you left?"

"Yes, but—"

Agent Maxwell raised his hand to stop me.

"Did you just see him, or did you two talk?"

"We talked."

"About what?"

"He apologized for being rude earlier in the evening."

"How was he rude?"

"I had inquired about his health, and he took it the wrong way."

"What kind of vehicle does he drive?"

"A maroon BMW."

"Texas or Illinois plates?"

"Texas."

Just then a man in a white coat walked in. "We need fiber

samples and fingerprints from all of the people who found the body," he said.

The agent clarified the request. "Since you touched the body, we need to exclude your presence from the analysis of the evidence."

"Sure."

When the technician had finished with me, the FBI agent told me I could go.

I headed back to Dean Simpson's office and knocked on the door.

"Come in," said Aris.

I opened the door, finding Aris sitting alone.

"Anything exciting happen?" asked Aris.

"Maxwell asked me a lot of questions about Lee. He seemed to have the impression from you that Lee had it in for Miles."

"I just told him what I remembered," said Aris. "One can't dispute the fact that Lee hated Miles, that Lee fantasized about smashing his skull, and that Lee's fantasy appears to have come true."

Chuck walked in without knocking.

"They seem to suspect your little Texas friend Lee as well as the New Millennium freaks," he said.

"It wasn't Lee."

"If not, they'll figure it out, but he sure had motive. Miles was the only thing standing between him and the *Review*."

I was starting to get pissed off. "Miles was the only thing standing between you and being editor-in-chief," I said.

Agents Zero and Maxwell walked back in.

"You're free to go home, but if you could stay by your phones, we'd appreciate it," said Zero.

"Does anyone need a ride?" I asked.

"Sure," said Chuck.

"Can I go to your place?" asked Aris.

"Of course," I said.

On our way out, we saw two FBI agents dusting the snow off of Lee's BMW, which had obviously spent the night at the law school.

SEVENTEEN

As Aris and I sat around my apartment waiting for some word on the FBI's investigation, it occurred to me that movies about police investigations are usually told from the investigator's perspective. So, as the investigator learns things, the viewer does too. I found it strange being on the dark side of the table, a party to an investigation, perhaps even the investigated. I knew virtually nothing. I didn't know who the agents were talking to or what they had found at the crime scene. I supposed, of course, that the agents had questioned Lee and that at some point Lee would call. Lee would probably finger me for revealing his thoughts about Miles—even though it was Aris who had been the leak. But I had told Aris and that was bad enough.

The phone rang.

"Hello," I said.

"You traitor!" shouted Lee.

"Calm down," I said.

"You told the FBI that I killed Miles."

"No, I didn't."

"That's what they told me."

"I swear I told them precisely the opposite."

"You're the only person I told."

"I mentioned it to Aris, and she—"

"That was personal. You had no business telling her—"

"I thought she might help you if she knew."

"The FBI read me my rights and then grilled me for two hours. They're talking about searching my apartment."

"They threatened all of us, trying to trip us up."

He hung up.

I supposed that I deserved Lee's scorn. After all, I shouldn't have told Aris in the first place.

"Who was that?" asked Aris.

"Lee."

"Did they question him?"

"After you blabbed about his fantasy, he's murder suspect number one," I said.

"Don't worry," she said. "It was a street crime, just like with old Rittinger."

"You think?" I hoped it was true.

"Come on, what self-respecting Texan would kill someone with a book? I mean, you've got three guns in your closet. The book thing is just too messy for anyone but a crack head."

The phone rang again.

"Hello."

"This is Chuck. Is Aris there?"

"Sure," I said, passing my cordless phone to Aris.

"Yeah," she said.

Pause.

"Thanks."

She clicked the phone off and handed it back to me.

"What's up?" I asked.

"Dean Simpson called Chuck. Some of the drawers had been rifled through at the *Review* office. The petty cash box is empty. Miles's watch and wallet are missing too."

"Crack head," I said.

"It could've just as easily been me there," said Aris, a tear escaping her eye.

I called Lee.

"Hello," he said.

"It looks like a crack head killed Miles."

"How do you know?"

"Simpson called Chuck. The petty cash was stolen. Miles's wallet is missing."

I heard a small yelp that had to be every nerve in Lee's body celebrating. "Thanks for the news. I'm going to take a nap."

"Bye then." I turned off the phone.

Aris put her arm around me. "I'm sorry if what I said… ."

"You had to be honest. If Lee had killed Miles, he would've deserved—"

"What if you thought that I had killed Miles?" interrupted Aris. She was frowning.

"Don't be absurd."

"I'm serious. What would you do?" she asked, stepping away from me.

"Lie. Like I did today."

"What do you mean?"

"The botched blackmail last night. I even said that I had heard Miles alive and well just before we left."

"How do you know about the blackmail?" she asked, folding her arms.

"I overheard your fight last night. Chuck was going to send the videotape around. Miles was going to press criminal charges against Chuck and you. There was going to be scorched earth at the *Law Review*."

"What were you, you ... listening at the door?"

"No, my cubicle is next to the far office, and the three of you were terribly loud."

"And you can actually hear conversations through the wall?"

"It's just dry board."

"Was there anyone else there with you?"

"No."

"Could anyone else have heard?"

"No."

"You're certain."

"Once you get past my table, you can't make out words."

"So you lied for me?" asked Aris. She took my hands in hers.

"Big time. The fact that you three had that vicious argument last night, and then the fact that I left Chuck and you alone with Miles for what—fifteen minutes."

"If you had told the FBI, we would've been detained, at least until they realized that the petty cash and Miles's wallet had been stolen. There might have even been a separate investigation into the blackmail."

"Do you think that Chuck could've gone back late last night?"

Aris dropped my hands and crossed her arms again.

The phone rang. "Hello."

"Chuck here. The dean called again. University police reported a strange, dark figure running from the law school around two this morning. They chased him into the neighborhood behind the law school, but he disappeared into an abandoned building."

"I'll tell Aris."

"Later." I turned off the phone.

"The university police chased a dark figure from the law school last night."

"Crude killing, theft, and a dark figure. Case closed," she said.

The phone rang.

"Hello?"

"Chuck here, again."

"Yeah."

"I almost forgot. Classes have been canceled tomorrow for a special memorial service. The dean said that at least two Supreme Court justices will attend. Put Aris on."

I passed her the phone.

She smiled broadly as Chuck talked.

When she hung up, she said, "We've been asked to address the memorial."

"Wow—"

"Take me," said Aris.

"Excuse me?"

"Just take me," she said.

Aris peeled off her sweat suit. "Take me, before… ."

I understood.

EIGHTEEN

The next morning Aris wanted to confer with Chuck over the content of their respective eulogies. I decided that I couldn't stomach the circus of Chuck and Aris firing script back and forth, so I dropped Aris off on the street and headed over to the law school. There were signs everywhere announcing the cancellation of classes and the memorial service. Half a dozen camera crews were interviewing students. I had to repeatedly decline their invitations.

Even with no classes, the law school was packed, perhaps even more packed than on an ordinary class day. People milled about in shock. Some women even appeared to be crying. Again and again, I heard the words: "It could've just as easily been me."

I saw stacks of the *Phoenix* with the headline: "LAW REVIEW EDITOR MURDERED IN OFFICE." I picked up a copy and found my way to a packed Green Lounge, taking a seat with a group of people I didn't know. I started to read, but I couldn't go on. I tossed the paper on the table and wandered over to the notice boards in the main foyer. There, in the *Law Review* section, were two crisp new letters.

The first read: "The *Law Review* is pleased to announce that Lee Randolph Gibbs has completed a substantial article. We welcome him to our staff."

The second read: "The *Law Review* has decided its appeal in *The Matter of Kupow*. Appeal denied."

Both letters were signed "Charles Hellar, editor-in-chief."

The decisions seemed rather fast on the heels of Miles's murder, but that was probably intentional. People were distracted by grief or fear. It was unlikely that the people who read the postings would pay them much thought. I grabbed a bite to eat from the Green Lounge snack bar and then headed over to the auditorium.

The two Supreme Court justices and Judge Vanderlyden were seated next to each other on the front row, surrounded by Agent Zero and friends. Panning the room, I found every seat full, except for some in the back. A bad seat is better than none at all.

Deans Simpson and Wolf, as well as half of the faculty, gave unqualified tribute to the academic work of William Miles Vanderlyden. When the professorate had finished, Chuck Hellar took the floor. Chuck's speech evoked the traditions of the school and the *Law Review*. He likened Miles to famous predecessors, including Dean Simpson. He spoke of how Miles had sought to uphold the traditions of the *Review* even in the face of great criticism and changing political times. "Conservatism," Chuck concluded, "is knowing what's too valuable to sacrifice at the altar of change. Without the leadership of William Miles Vanderlyden, the *Law Review* would not be what it is today."

Loud applause.

Aris was next. Her speech took a different approach. She explained how, over the course of their arduous *Law Review* work, Miles and she had become best of friends, like the brother she never had. She lamented that "people often overlook the personal relationships that develop in close working environments." Those relationships, she explained, "are the true soul of the *Law Review*." Her sentimental speech concluded with "I loved William Miles Vanderlyden."

Immense applause.

In tears, Judge Vanderlyden met Aris at the podium and thanked the crowd. The woman sitting next to me commented: "She's that rare person who's both sensitive and successful." I nodded. Aris had become the true beneficiary of Miles's demise. Brilliant tactics, Aris.

I waited until the crowd dispersed and then started toward the library. Agent Zero caught up with me in the hall.

"Mr. Bullock, would you mind answering a few more questions?"

"Of course not."

I followed him back to another small administrative office.

When we were seated, I asked, "What's this about?"

"We want to tie up a few loose ends, that's all."

"Based on what I've heard about the thefts and the dark figure, it sounds like there are no loose ends."

"The loose end that I'm concerned about at this moment is one Mr. Gibbs."

"What?"

"His prints match those on a plastic Coke bottle that was set atop of a trash can in the *Law Review* office where Vanderlyden was murdered."

"He probably left it there on one of his visits to the *Review* office to talk about his article."

"He claims he hasn't been there in several days. The janitors empty the trash every weeknight. That means that Lee was there, at the scene, sometime between late Friday night and the time of the murder." He clicked his pen.

"Perhaps he touched the bottle downstairs at the snack bar but bought another. Then someone else bought the bottle and took it to the *Review* office."

"His were the only recognizable prints on the bottle."

I was silent.

"What was Mr. Gibbs's demeanor two nights ago?" asked Zero.

"Like I said before, he looked tired, exhausted."

"Nervous?"

"Not any more than usual."

"So he's usually a nervous person," said Zero, taking some notes.

"Lately, because there was this looming question of his future."

"Well, that little problem was solved today. Mr. Gibbs became part of *Law Review*." He smiled and clicked his pen. "How convenient."

"I know."

"I've heard time and again how important this *Law Review* is. But it can't make you famous, can't make you rich. Why would seemingly rational and bright students put everything on the line to get on a journal run by a self-selected triad of students?"

"Lee didn't kill Miles to get on the *Review*. And you're right. The *Law Review* just isn't important enough to kill someone over it."

"That's what I thought at first, but I'm troubled," said Zero, "troubled by the attitude here. Why would you want to be on the *Review*?"

"Well, I'd like to clerk for a U.S. Court of Appeals Judge, and I probably can't do that without being on the *Review*."

"Why do you want a job that pays $30,000 a year when law firms pay first-year attorneys almost $100,000?"

"It's not always about money. Beyond riches, there is power. Isn't that why you're an FBI agent?"

"How much power can one of these clerks really wield? What do they do, file court orders?"

"Clerks write the first draft of every legal opinion and pick all of the laws to support the decision of the court. They help create precedent and thereby shape the outcome of future cases."

"I understand it's also a stepping stone to other positions," said Zero.

"Doing the same thing for the Supreme Court."

"Even more power," said Zero, clicking his pen.

"Each of these positions leads to something greater. Supreme Court clerks go on to other powerful jobs at the Department of Justice and the White House, eventually, perhaps, to become judges themselves."

"So everyone here is obsessed with obtaining such positions?"

"I wouldn't use the word obsessed."

"Is that what everyone wants?"

"Not everyone. Different people want different careers."

"But what about Lee?"

"Yes, but not enough to kill someone for it."

"I've investigated cases where people killed for far less than what you've just described. Is it possible that Gibbs just lost his perspective, went crazy even?"

"I saw him fairly close to the time Miles was killed, and he wasn't crazy"

"When did you see Mr. Gibbs last?"

"Around ten on Sunday evening."

"When you left, then, Mr. Gibbs and Mr. Vanderlyden were both still in the library?"

"To the best of my knowledge, yes."

"Did Mr. Gibbs ever mention to you that he slept in the library?"

"Yes."

"You may go," said Zero. He shooed me as if I were some insect.

I stood up and walked to the door.

"Is this case closed or not?" I asked, turning back around.

"It won't be closed until we've caught our killer."

"Wouldn't your efforts be better spent in tracking down Professor Rittinger's assailant?"

"We did that yesterday."

"Why haven't you arrested him, then?"

"He's serving three to five in Indiana. Just after he robbed Rittinger, he tried to buy drugs from an undercover officer in Gary. He's been in jail ever since."

"What about the other crack heads?"

"We're working on them. Judge Vanderlyden has offered a $500,000 reward. At this moment, Chicago police officers are explaining to every crack head in this part of Chicago how much rock $500,000 will buy. If one of these people did in Vanderlyden, someone will talk." He clicked his pen again.

"It wasn't Lee," I said.

I left, thinking Chuck a much more likely suspect than Lee. Surely, Chuck could have walked back in the snow later that night, knowing full well that Miles would be working until the small hours of the morning. Chuck had the editor-in-chief's position to gain, a certain Supreme Court clerkship, and of course, to the extent Chuck truly cared, control over the *Review*. Chuck also might have had a great deal to lose if Miles had sought to expose the blackmail. I wasn't sure whether what Miles and Aris had attempted was illegal, but Miles's father was certainly powerful. An aggressive district attorney could probably put a creative spin on a number of federal statutes and pin something on them.

That evening I confided in Aris my continuing suspicion of Chuck. She burst out laughing, assuring me that if Chuck had wanted to destroy Miles, he would have done so in a much more painful manner, with the videotape. Or better yet, she queried, why destroy Miles at all? She said that they both believed that Miles would capitulate to their demands after he had slept on the ramifications of the videotape's exposure. As underhanded as Chuck was, she stressed, his tactics were more sophisticated than violence.

NINETEEN

The next night Aris moved into my apartment on the pretext of helping me study for final exams. While I suppose Miles's murder could have distracted me from the task at hand, the result was the opposite. Studying became a way to escape the investigation. I suppose that I was Aris's outlet too: a new project to be tackled with as much resolve as she approached everything else.

Yet the investigation went on in the background of our lives. Lee's father had sent a big-shot criminal defense lawyer up from Dallas to deal with the FBI. Lee was eventually questioned in the presence of his attorney, but after that, the FBI's interest in Lee appeared to wane.

By exam week, it seemed that the whole school had forgotten about Miles. People were studying around the clock and planning their Christmas vacations. I was to fly home to Houston, and Aris was off to Virginia to see her father. It would be nice to get away from this town, from its oppressive cold, from its lack of sunlight.

I studied particularly hard the two days before my civil procedure exam, taking abbreviated versions of exams that had been given in previous years. Aris would then check my answers against the two or three answers that had received the highest grades in those prior years, which were made public by professors and filed in the library.

I finally took my civil procedure exam on the morning of December 16—three hours long, hardly enough time to answer every question. Nonetheless, I felt like I had identified and adequately discussed all of the legal issues.

After the exam, I was far too tired to study, but early the next morning, I hit my elements of law outlines hard in preparation for Bliston's exam. That afternoon and evening, I took three old elements exams. While Aris graded my answers, I reviewed my outline one last time.

At 9:00 the next morning, I sat for my last exam of the quarter, elements of the law. Aris had anticipated all but one of the questions, and I walked out of the exam elated. I was even happier when I found Aris waiting for me in the hall. She put her arm in mine and gently pulled me from the dazed procession.

"Come with me now and don't ask any questions," she said with a look of panic.

"What?"

"Just come with me."

"Okay," I said, following her. I half expected some sexual favor, but her body language conveyed fear rather than pleasure.

Her Saab was illegally parked in front of the law school. Its flashers were on.

"Get in."

I did.

Aris pulled out quickly, looking around and into her mirrors, as if she expected someone would be following her.

"So where are we going?"

"The airport."

"Excuse me?"

"Merry Christmas and Happy No More Exam Day!" she said, laughing.

"What?"

"I'm taking you to Hawaii."

"But I'm supposed to fly to Houston tomorrow to visit my parents."

"You can call them from Hawaii."

"What about clothes?" I asked.

"Already packed," said Aris. "Look in the back seat."

There were two carry-on garment bags in the back seat, one of which I recognized as my own.

"Ah-ha," I said.

Aris headed away from Lake Shore Drive and through Washington Park, just west of the law school.

"Why are we going this way?" I asked.

"Short cut." We exited the park into a mire of abandoned buildings and housing projects.

"Lovely."

"You've never cut across to the Dan Ryan?" asked Aris.

"No, and it's not too difficult to see why."

My heart slowed once we were out of the projects and on the Ryan Expressway, but quickened again as Aris whipped in and out of traffic. I glanced over at the speedometer: ninety-plus.

"Is there a reason you're driving like—"

"Our flight leaves in an hour."

"Let's hope the Kennedy isn't backed up," I said.

"We'll see. If it is, we'll take the Ike."

As we approached the spaghetti-bowl where the Dan Ryan, Kennedy, Stevenson, and Eisenhower Expressways converge just south of the Sears Tower, we could see brake lights ahead in all the lanes exiting to the Kennedy.

"Hold on," said Aris. "It looks like we're taking the Ike."

Aris darted across eight lanes of traffic to the far right lane, which was moving smoothly.

We took a sharp curve and then headed west from downtown on I-290, the Eisenhower Expressway.

Thanks to Aris's driving, we arrived at our gate with a few minutes to spare. A long boarding line was still snaking its way through the terminal. I sucked in the deepest breath I could, but my heart was still pounding from the sprint across Terminal One. We checked in and then joined the end of the line. We didn't speak again until we had taken our seats in first class, on the upper deck of a 747.

"I'll take the aisle," said Aris.

I slid in front of Aris and took the window seat.

A stewardess arrived. "Champagne?"

"I'll pass," said Aris.

"Sure," I said.

While I sipped my champagne, I looked out the window and into the terminal. For a moment, I thought I saw Chuck and his white hair in the waiting area inside the terminal, but when I blinked my eyes, the figure was gone.

"I thought I just saw Chuck," I said.

"Excuse me?" asked Aris, looking out my window.

"I looked over at the terminal, and I thought I saw Chuck inside."

"Let's trade seats," said Aris, standing.

I got up, and Aris slid behind me.

"Just relax and go to sleep," she said, looking out the window.

Exhausted, I slept until the plane took a sharp turn on its final approach into Honolulu. Looking beyond Aris and out her window, I could see the lush green of Oahu and the deep blue of the Pacific. At Honolulu, we transferred to a small commuter plane, which took us on to our final destination, the little island of Lanai.

"This is loud," I shouted in Aris's ear, as the little plane rumbled along over the blue Pacific.

"Yeah."

I stared out the window at the blue ocean, until a small island came into view. It was reddish brown on the side facing us, and then bright green toward the middle.

"That's Lanai," said Aris, pointing.

As we passed over the near-side of the shore, I saw two rusted freighters shipwrecked against the island's reef.

I pointed to the boats.

Aris shouted, "Shipwreck Beach."

I nodded.

The plane banked hard to the right and then again to the left.

I could see the little landing strip directly ahead of us through the captain's open cockpit.

There was a rough jolt as we touched down, but we slowed quickly, finally stopping in front of a small building.

After the captain opened the doorway, we descended the steps of the plane into a crowd of hotel employees, who showered us with flowers.

"Manele Bay guests over here, in the van," said a white-clothed man.

We boarded the van, which promptly departed. The drive to the hotel was a precarious, twisting descent, and it afforded spectacular views of the bay and the majestic hotel that graced its shores.

"That's our place?" I asked.

"It sure is," sighed Aris.

"Are there private beaches?"

"Oh, yes." She squeezed my thigh.

Upon arrival, we were greeted with warm towels and escorted to our small suite, which had a balcony overlooking the bay in the distance as well as the hotel's Hawaiian garden immediately below.

I tried to kiss Aris.

"Not now."

"Oh, I'm sorry," I said, surprised at her disinterest. "Are you okay?"

"I'm just not in the mood yet. Let's get some food and go to bed early."

Unfortunately, by bed she meant not sex, but mere sleep.

TWENTY

We rose early the next morning and enjoyed breakfast on our balcony during which we battled rainbow-colored tropical birds for the muffins in our bread basket. We eventually abandoned our food to the birds, slopped sun screen all over each other, and slipped into swimsuits. I had on red-and-blue-striped Polo shorts. Aris was devastating in her sleek, white one-piece with mesh shoulder straps.

We wandered down through the Hawaiian garden, past the pool area, and onto the path to the beach. The path itself was made of sharp volcanic pumice and was not at all suitable for bare feet. Consequently, I ended up carrying Aris the last fifty yards of the path, until it ended on a white, half-moon beach, bordered by gently swaying palms. Wave after wave made a relaxing swish upon the sand.

"Welcome to Manele Bay. I see that you are new arrivals, yes?" said a hotel employee.

We both nodded.

"I'm the cabana boy. I arrange food, drinks, snorkeling equipment—"

Aris interrupted, "Snorkeling equipment. Yes, we'd like two sets, please."

"Yes, ma'am," the boy said. "Let me look at your feet."

We each lifted our left foot in the boy's direction.

"I'll be right back."

The boy shuffled off into the palms and toward a cabana.

While we waited, I noticed that Aris seemed a little wired.

"Are you all right?" I asked, touching her shoulder.

"Oh, yeah." She forced a smile.

The first boy sent another companion with two white towels and two little blue-and-white-striped beach chairs. "Where would you like to sit?" he asked, panting slightly.

"Right over there," said Aris, pointing to a spot about halfway between the palms and the breaking waves.

"Yes, ma'am."

Cabana boy number two set up both chairs with towels across their backs.

We had just started to walk toward our chairs when cabana boy number one arrived with our snorkeling equipment.

"I brought floatation belts just in case," he said.

"Thanks," I said.

"Don't enter the bay on this side of the beach—lots of black urchins," he said, pointing to the right.

"Excuse me?" I asked.

"I've been here before," said Aris, dismissing him with her hand.

"Yes, ma'am."

"Urchins are cute little pointy things, right?" I asked.

"Have you ever snorkeled before?" asked Aris.

"No," I said.

"Well, Hawaiian snorkel rule number one: don't touch anything."

"Okay, but what in particular should I be—"

"Sea urchins, coral, eels, and shells," she said, walking toward our lounges. I followed.

"What do you mean by shells?"

"Like you would buy in a shell store, particularly the ones with a cone shape. They bite if provoked."

I nodded.

"I've spent enough time here with my dad that I can find my way around this bay without ever having to lift my head above water. So long as you leave the marine life alone, it leaves you alone."

"Let's hit it then," I said.

Aris grabbed my hand and led me to the far left end of the half-moon beach, supposedly the end without sea urchins. We slipped into our flippers and masks. I also donned a waist float, but Aris laughed when I suggested that she wear one as well.

"Follow me," said Aris, lunging headfirst into an incoming wave and propelling herself several feet from shore.

I did the same, hitting the surprisingly cool water with a splash. When I tried to breathe through my snorkel, I managed to inhale the better part of a wave. I pulled the snorkel from my mouth, coughing and dog paddling in search of air. Even with my head above water, the cool water was making me hyperventilate. I wasn't just paddling like a dog, I was panting like one.

Aris swam up beside me and removed her snorkel. "Are you drowning?"

"Cold."

"You'll get used to it in about five minutes," she said. Then she replaced her snorkel and headed off into deeper water without me.

I put my snorkel back into my mouth and placed my face in the water. Before me lay a crystal aquarium filled with countless species of fish, large and small, long and skinny, short and fat, some shaped like diamonds, some with long, sharp fins, others with big, floppy fins. They comprised every color imaginable—yellow, orange, black, white, red, blue, green. I could hear myself moaning in delight.

Looking further out into the bay, I could see Aris's graceful legs mingling with a school of giant angel fish. Below us, towers of coral rose from the sandy floor like surrealist chess pieces. I passed just two feet or so above one and looked down to see four basketball-sized orange sea urchins. Thick appendages dangled off in my direction. I swam madly, concerned that they might attack at any moment.

I explored the bay like that for an hour, chasing an octopus here, a moray eel there, all the while surrounded by fish that must have been close to three feet long. When I finally pulled my tired body out of the bay and onto the beach, I felt unusually heavy, almost missing the freedom and buoyancy of the salty Pacific. I walked over to our towels and collapsed into my chair, reminded of my athletic mediocrity.

I watched Aris climb out two hours later. Her sheer white suit left her, for all practical purposes, completely nude.

When she reached me, I tossed her a towel. "I love your swimsuit," I said.

"My waifish-figure looks horrid in lined suits."

"Shall we go upstairs?"

"Only if you carry me up."

I did, but about halfway up the path, I thought I saw Chuck on the balcony of a room.

I stopped and squinted.

The man immediately turned and went inside, but I saw that he had curly white hair.

I noticed that Aris had been looking at the same balcony.

"What are you looking at?" she asked.

"A bird," I said, half convinced that I was losing it.

"What color was it?"

"I couldn't tell. It was flying too near the sun."

Much to my disappointment, we didn't consummate our trip to Hawaii that afternoon or evening. I could tell something was bothering Aris and that she was uncomfortable. I'm sure she would have let me make love to her had I pushed the issue. But I didn't think her heart would be in it, so I decided to wait.

* * *

The next day we awoke at dawn and rented a jeep to explore the outer, more private reaches of the island. Our first destination was Polihua Beach, a nearly inaccessible stretch of sand looking out onto Molokai. The drive to Polihua was, in a word, arduous—bouncing over the remnants of a collapsed volcano crater, a foreboding landscape of red and purple rock that looked more like Death Valley than Hawaii. After about an hour, we pulled in under some trees and parked at the edge of the sandy beach, which descended steeply into ferocious white waves of eight feet or more.

"We're alone," said Aris. She hopped out of the jeep and pulled off her shorts, t-shirt, bikini top, and even, bikini bottom. As I was slipping out of my trunks, Aris bolted down the beach, frolicking and spinning and kicking sand. I gave chase.

After about fifty yards of sprinting, Aris finally slowed, and I caught up, tackling her into the soft sand. We wrestled, rolling down the incline of the beach, kissing and rubbing against each other until we were making love in the cold foam of the breaking waves. Just as we were about to complete our coupling, a giant wave covered us, dispatching us out into the Pacific like pieces of driftwood. We continued our lovemaking in the water, twisting together in the open ocean until we had our much anticipated release.

Separating, I watched as Aris's body moved away from me in the clear water, rising and falling on huge swells. One second I was looking downhill at Aris's head, the next at her treading legs through the side of a transparent wave.

"Are we going to die?" I asked.

"No, we just have to be careful to ride one of these waves into shore. I've swum here before, and the waves are always pretty big."

As we ascended to the crest of a large wave, I saw a giant sea creature surface about twenty yards away.

"What was that? A shark?"

"Too big for a shark. A whale I think."

I realized that I was using a lot of energy in the waves and that I was getting tired. "Let's go back to shore," I suggested.

"Just stay next to me," said Aris, swimming to my side. "Approach the shore with your hands out in front of your head. Whatever you do, don't let your head hit the sand. Break your landing with your hands and try to body surf up as high on the beach as possible. Once on the beach, scamper on all fours up the slope."

I swam a modified version of the breast stroke toward shore with my head above water.

"Wait right here for a big one," said Aris, grabbing my arm.

We were in a trough.

"No, not this one," she said as we rose up the crest of the next wave.

Back into a trough.

"Now!" yelled Aris, paddling madly. I followed her lead.

We rose atop a giant wave that gradually collapsed beneath us until I felt the sand of Polihua.

The undertow was strong, trying to pull me back out with the wave, but I dug my hands and feet into the sand. When the tugging stopped, I scampered uphill, just barely escaping the next wave.

Aris was already waiting for me, sitting at the top of the beach. While she relaxed, I fetched our picnic basket from the jeep. We unfurled the red-and-white checked blanket and enjoyed fish sandwiches while a family of Humpback whales took turns breaching and flailing their tails at us just off shore.

After lunch we continued our circumnavigation of the island, driving through the rain forest on Lanai's windward side. Dense jungle surrounded us and a constant rain of sweet-smelling flowers fell into the Jeep as we negotiated the muddy road. The highlight of the drive occurred when the jungle cover broke to reveal a deep canyon filled with a giant rainbow. We parked the jeep and made love at the lip of the canyon. We lingered there all afternoon, caressing each other until sunset.

As we drove back to our hotel in the darkness, I thought I was happier than I had ever been.

TWENTY-ONE

Later that night, Aris and I tended to our respective sunburns, particularly those parts unused to sunlight. When we finished our travel-sized bottle of aloe, Aris sent me to the hotel gift shop for more. There, I looked at the t-shirts, hats, and Hawaiian souvenirs for about twenty minutes before returning to our room. I opened the hotel door expecting to see only Aris, but I found Chuck as well.

"Why, hello," said Chuck, red as a beet. His white hair looked even whiter against his sunburn.

"Chuck has decided to join us," said Aris, sitting topless at the edge of the bed.

"I hope you have your own room." I wanted to vomit.

"It overlooks the trail leading down to the beach," said Chuck, smiling.

"I know," I said.

"I'm off," said Chuck, "but I do hope that you'll be able to join Aris and me on our snorkeling expedition tomorrow."

He brushed past me, and I slammed the door behind him.

"Let me explain—" said Aris.

"I can't imagine how." I grabbed her arm.

"Would you believe me if I told you that he had planned to come here months ago?" She twisted her arm free.

"Why's he here?"

"He's in love with me."

"What?"

"Like I said, he's in love with me." She laid back on the bed.

"I thought—"

"He's obsessed with me."

"So why do you tolerate—"

"The same reason you do."

"How can he even afford to come here? What are you doing, subsidizing him?"

She looked away.

I left the room, walked down to the beach, and sat alone in the darkness. I watched the white lines of breaking waves roll in, one after another. I wondered whether I'd ever be able to have Aris to myself. I lost track of time, and when I returned to the room, Aris was sound asleep. I climbed into bed beside her and clung to the edge, not even wanting to touch her. That night I slept uneasily, dreaming constantly of them having sex, and of Aris running her delicate fingers through Chuck's thick hair.

* * *

I awoke to the loud ringing of the telephone, which I answered clumsily.

"Rise and shine, it's snorkeling time," said Chuck.

It was 7:30.

"I'm going back to sleep," I said, trying to hang up the phone.

Aris pulled the phone away from me. "When shall we meet you?"

Pause.

"Fine. Eight it is."

Aris rolled out of bed and headed for the shower.

I was in an awkward position. Either I go along with Chuck and endure his meddling, or I hang around here and let Chuck have Aris all to himself. Of course, I opted for accompanying them. So long as I was on this island, I was going to be with Aris—Chuck or no Chuck. He was not going to have an opportunity to sleep with her because they were not going to be alone.

We met Chuck in the hotel lobby at eight and hopped into his jeep. I got in the back, while Aris sat in the front passenger seat.

"Do you have three sets of gear?" asked Aris.

"Of course," said Chuck, patting her thigh.

The jeep climbed up the mountain, passed through the little village of Lanai City, and then descended the other side of the island.

"That's Maui," said Aris, pointing to an island in the distance.

I also could see one of the hulking shipwrecks just offshore.

"So where are we going?" I asked.

"Shipwreck Beach," said Aris.

"It's suitable for snorkeling?"

"Perfectly," she said. "I've been there before without incident."

"We're going there to see the giant sea turtles," said Chuck.

"I didn't know you were into snorkeling," I said.

"This is my first trip to the tropics," said Chuck. "I've been taking lessons these last two days, but I'm getting better."

When we were at sea level, Chuck turned off of the paved road and onto the beach. Looking out, the water was virtually placid for about fifty yards, where I could see a line of waves breaking over what I suspected was a reef of some kind. Up the coast, I could see the giant rusted tankers.

Aris pulled out a pair of binoculars and started scanning the horizon.

"What are you looking for?" I asked.

"Turtles. When they come up for air, you can see them."

We had driven a few miles closer to the tankers when Aris yelled, "There's one. Stop!"

Chuck brought the jeep to a quick stop.

I strained for a glimpse of the turtle, but couldn't see anything but a large sailboat well offshore.

"Mind if I use your binoculars?" I asked.

Aris passed them to me.

I looked for the turtle but saw nothing. I then zeroed in on the sailboat. A man and a woman were on deck, eating. They were pretty far away. I panned over to the nearest tanker. The waves looked even larger when juxtaposed against the tanker, perhaps ten feet or more.

"Enough peeping," said Chuck, pulling the binoculars away and replacing them with two flippers, a snorkel, and a mask.

"The turtle's going to get away," said Aris, as she jumped from the jeep.

"Don't you have a floater belt?" I asked.

"Can't you swim?" asked Chuck.

"You won't be able to chase after turtles with a floater belt," said Aris, wading into the lagoon.

I tried not to look scared, but I was.

Chuck and I followed Aris into the water. The three of us were soon paddling away toward where Aris had last seen the turtle. Looking down, the bottom of the lagoon was sandy with intermittent patches of coral. There were fish, but not nearly as many as there had been in the bay by the hotel.

Aris and Chuck, better swimmers, were a bit ahead of me, and I sped up, trying to catch them. They finally stopped, and I saw Aris pointing downward. I followed her hand to a dog-sized turtle, which was gliding effortlessly over the coral. As the turtle used its flippers to steer through the coral formations, my overwhelming impression was of grace. Aris tapped me on the shoulder, and I surfaced.

"Was that the one you saw?" asked Chuck.

"No, the one I saw was at least six feet. It's got to be around here somewhere," said Aris.

"There it is!" yelled Chuck, pointing toward where the waves were breaking against the barrier reef.

I could see a wake in the water, just before the reef.

"First one of you to find the turtle gets to spend the night with me," said Aris.

My gut hurt with a sinking panic. Before I had regained my composure, Chuck was already headed off toward the turtle. I paused just long enough to remember which way the turtle had been swimming, and then took a slightly different heading than Chuck. I swam as fast as I could and hardly noticed a large moray eel that twisted by me. My gaze was focused off into the distant depths, looking for the turtle.

I had been swimming for fifteen minutes when I realized that the water was becoming shallower, much shallower. The coral was immediately beneath me, and there was no sign of the turtle. I brought my head to the surface and saw that I was just ten yards from the breaking surf and the open ocean beyond. I turned around, put my face in the water, and headed back. I had moved but a few feet when the fish below me disappeared in a blur of sand. The current had me too, pulling me backwards, out to sea. I tried to swim against the riptide, but it was useless. At the last possible moment, I spun around and swam into the towering waves, hoping to cross the reef between swells. Just when I thought that I would make it over the reef, a wave collapsed on top of me, twisting me in its foam.

When I came to the surface, I was treading on the crest of a large swell several yards beyond the surf, in open water. I dropped down into a trough and could see only blue around me. I rose up again, and I looked back toward shore, trying to spot Aris and Chuck. They were nowhere to be seen.

"Help!" I yelled as I descended into another trough.

Then I remembered the sailboat. When I rose atop the next crest, I turned and could see the sailboat. It wasn't that far.

"Help!" I yelled in the direction of the boat.

I swam toward the sailboat, but even though I couldn't feel a current, I was being pulled further up the coast, away from the sailboat, and out to sea.

"Help!" I yelled again, in the direction of the sailboat, this time flailing my arms as well.

I couldn't see anyone on deck.

My legs were getting numb. I couldn't stay afloat forever, particularly using this much energy, so I tried to relax and float on my back. I waited for every crest, at which point I yelled and flailed my arms. Death seemed imminent and just as I thought of the *Waste Land's* drowned sailor, something was on top of me, pulling me up from the water.

"Are you all right?" I heard a man asking.

"Yeah," I rattled. My voice was hoarse from screaming.

The stranger rolled me over onto my back. I ascertained that I was in a dinghy of some kind. I could hear its motor purring and revving, and then everything went black.

* * *

I awoke to the face of a breathtaking blonde. I was certain I was dead.

"You're lucky to be alive," she said.

I coughed and felt sharp twinges of pain in both legs. She was right. I reached for my legs.

"No, no," said the woman, grabbing my wrists. "Don't touch."

I was on my back, so I pulled myself up slightly to get a look at my legs. There was a deep, oozing cut about six inches long just above my right knee. Several, smaller cuts covered my left shin and foot.

"What happened?"

"The coral on the fringe reef," she said.

"Where are we?"

"Heading for Manele Bay. We'll be there in about thirty minutes. But we're sailing headlong into a Kona."

"A what?" The boat was pitching quite a bit.

"A Kona storm is on its way, kicking up surf, and bringing strong winds. It's essentially a Hawaiian winter storm. It'll rain, the wind will blow a bit, and there will be huge waves."

"Is that what caused the riptide?"

"It probably made it worse, but there's always a riptide along Shipwreck Beach. It's caused by the ocean currents passing between Maui and Lanai. That's why no one ever swims there. Even on the calmest of days, the current can sweep you halfway to the Cook Islands before anyone realizes you're missing."

"But don't people go there to look at the turtles?" I asked.

"We've been moored in Manele Bay for seven months, circumnavigated the island countless times, and I've never seen a human being in the water off Shipwreck Beach. Every map to the island warns against swimming there."

The door flung open. "Mommy, mommy, mommy," said a little golden-haired boy.

"Thomas meet, Mr.—I'm sorry," she said.

"Hello, Thomas, I'm Grayson Bullock."

"Is he dead?" asked the boy.

"Not yet," I said.

"Is he going to die?" he persisted, poking at my toes.

"No," said the woman, laughing.

"The man was your husband?" I asked.

"Yes. My name's Evelyn, Evelyn Davis, and my husband, Archer, pulled you from the ocean."

"I think I need a hospital." I was afraid the child's question might come true.

"The Lanai doctor is meeting us at the pier and taking you to his clinic to stitch those up."

"My friends?" I asked, remembering Aris and Chuck. "Did they make it out of the current?"

"The ones in the jeep?" she asked.

"Yes."

"They were both driving away when we saw you yelling."

"Oh."

"I'm going to go take care of Thomas now, if you don't mind."

I nodded, and they left me alone in the room. I lay there for half an hour, getting queasy as the boat pitched to and fro, afraid to ask myself why Aris had let Chuck take us to Shipwreck Beach.

At the dock, we were met by an ambulance, which was driven by the island doctor. He took me back to a small shack in Lanai City. "Lanai Hospital and Clinic" was hand-painted on it in large white letters. There, the doctor cleaned up my wounds, stitched the big cut, wrapped everything in gauze, and poked me with a couple of shots. He also gave me a bottle of pain pills and a pair of crutches.

"The hotel bus will pick you up there," he said pointing to a little shed.

"What do I owe you?" I asked.

"I'll just bill it to your room."

The little bus that runs between the hotel and the airport picked me up about ten minutes later.

By the time I got back to the Manele Bay, it was dark and raining. I hobbled along the walkway to my room, trying to stay in the middle so the blowing rain wouldn't wet my bandages. When I reached my room, I felt for my wallet and key, but of course, I'd left them in the jeep.

I banged on the door.

"Coming," I heard Aris say.

The door opened. She hugged me and started to cry.

"Watch out for my legs," I said.

Aris backed away. Streams of tears were running from her red and puffy eyes. It looked as if she had been crying for some time.

"They wouldn't tell me how bad you were hurt, only that you had been taken to the hospital."

"I'm fine. I just needed my cuts stitched-up and bandaged. The coral."

Aris hugged me again, leaning forward so as not to touch my legs.

"Lie down," she said, though I could hardly hear her through all the crying.

She took my crutches and then helped me to lift my legs up on the bed.

Becoming more and more aware of the pain in my legs, I remembered the pain pills in my pocket. I pulled out the bottle, popped one out, and swallowed it without any water.

"Why did you take us there? You knew how dangerous it was."

"Excuse me?"

"Didn't you say you'd snorkeled at Shipwreck?"

"I had," said Aris.

"Did you know it was dangerous?"

"I knew there's a current by the reef—"

"But you didn't tell me?"

"I thought—"

"You practically told me to swim into the reef."

"I didn't warn you about getting too close to where the waves were breaking because it was obviously dangerous."

"I didn't swim to where the waves were breaking. The strongest riptide imaginable pulled me there. The current tore me through the reef and then carried me a mile out to sea."

"I didn't feel it," she said, climbing in bed with me.

I stared into Aris's eyes, trying to figure out whether she was telling the truth.

"You didn't injure this, did you?" she asked, pulling my

swim trunks down just far enough.

I closed my eyes and tried to forget, and trust.

TWENTY-TWO

When I awoke the next morning to searing pain, Aris was over me immediately with a pill and a glass of water. Our bags were packed and neatly arranged in the middle of the room.

"Are we leaving?" I asked, rubbing my eyes.

"Yes."

"When's our flight?"

"Noon."

I looked at my watch: 8:28.

"Then I can go back to sleep." I closed my eyes.

"But our flight leaves from Maui, and that means we've got to take the nine o'clock ferry."

"Huh?"

"The Lanai airport is closed because of the storm. It may be closed for days."

"Oh." I climbed out of bed and got dressed.

When the bellman arrived, we followed him to a packed bus waiting in front of the hotel. The drive was short, just around the bay to the harbor. The Davis boat was moored there, but no one was on deck.

Aris and I, being the last on the bus, were also the first off.

We proceeded directly to a small ferry, which had twenty wooden pews split by a center aisle. Only about half of the pews were inside the cabin. The rest were open air. We boarded, and Aris helped me to a centrally located seat inside the cabin.

"Excuse me," she said to a crew member, "is this the large ferry?"

"No."

"I bought tickets for the large ferry," she said.

"The large ferry hit a rock in the storm this morning. It's this or nothing." He walked on to the front cabin.

While most of the busload was able to scrunch into the cabin, about half a dozen men were relegated to the outside seats. The captain spoke to the crowd: "It was rough on the ride over from Maui. It'll be much of the same on the ride back. Find your seats and don't try to move."

The captain fired up the engines. The little ferry backed up, turned sharply, and chugged along at a smooth pace toward the mouth of the harbor. When we came around the little point that protected the harbor, we hit our first big wave. The ferry made a creaking sound, pitched a good forty-five degrees sideways, and then came crashing down with a splash that covered the entire boat, soaking the uncovered passengers on the back.

This continued as we inched our way toward Maui in twelve-foot seas. Within ten minutes, Aris and I were sick, along with most of the other passengers. There weren't any vomit bags or open windows so everyone vomited onto the white steel floor of the ferry. The closed cabin reeked, and I almost wished for an outside seat. Aris and I hiked our shirts up over our faces to use as masks. Even worse than the smell was the floor. A thick, sticky stew sloshed back and forth as the ship's center of gravity changed. Despite placing our feet upon the back of the pew in front of us, we would still get splashed when the ship took a particularly vicious roll. There was nothing more we could do.

After thirty minutes of this torture, we finally arrived in Lahaina, Maui. We proceeded immediately to the nearest beachwear store. We bought new clothes and shoes, changed in the dressing room, and disposed of their stinking predecessors in a trash barrel.

"Let's get a cab to airport," said Aris.

"I really don't feel up to flying."

"You'll feel better by the time we get to the airport."

"Why don't we spend a few nights here?"

"My flight to Virginia leaves Chicago tomorrow. The day after that is Christmas Eve. All the later flights are sold out. If I don't leave now, I can't be with my dad on Christmas."

"Why don't you go on without me, then," I suggested.

"Are you sure?"

"I can take care of myself."

"Here's your ticket, then," she said, handing me an envelope.

I carried her bags over to a cab parked at the ferry dock and helped her inside.

"I love you," she said.

"I love you, too."

After we kissed, I closed the door and watched her drive off.

I checked into a cheap motel with a room overlooking the harbor. The ferry was already gone, making another run to Lanai. About two hours later, I heard the ferry's diesel engine again and went to the window. Sure enough, Chuck was the first to disembark, carrying a tattered yellow shoulder bag. He jumped in a cab and headed off, presumably chasing after Aris.

I stayed in the old whaling village until after Christmas, brooding over the possibility that the snorkeling trip to Shipwreck Beach might have been concocted by Chuck, maybe even Aris as well. Aris had not denied that she had paid for Chuck's ticket and room. She was the one who knew the island and had sent me into the reef.

"First one of you to find the turtle. . . ."
"First one of you to find the turtle. . . ."
"First one of you to find the turtle. . . ."

I tried to remember where they were when I was pulled into the reef. They were far from the reef, far from where we had seen the turtle. Why would they wish to hurt me, though? I pondered again the possibility that Chuck had returned to the law school late that Sunday and had killed Miles. I was the only witness to their argument and the attempted blackmail. But Chuck didn't know that I had overheard their meeting, unless, of course, Aris had told him. Quite likely, I thought. Could she have participated in Miles's murder? She was with me the whole night, but I thought of her staying upstairs with Chuck for several minutes while I waited in the parking lot. I tried to remember how long they had been up there.

Was my imagination running wild? Is it possible that they killed Miles for Supreme Court clerkships? They already had important clerkships on the U.S. Court of Appeals and permanent job offers from one of the most powerful law firms in Washington, D.C. Their success was stratospheric. It seemed inconceivable that they would risk so much. Then I thought of Chuck's angry ramblings at the Four Seasons, his contorted blackmail scheme, and of course, Lee's murderous fantasies. Nothing seemed to make sense anymore.

TWENTY-THREE

Aris arrived back in Chicago from Virginia the same day I flew in from Hawaii. We took a cab to my apartment and relaxed there for the rest of the week, renting movies and waiting for 1993. On New Year's Eve we went to a party at the Chicago Athletic Association. I wore my black tuxedo again. Aris had on a stunning silver-sequined dress that descended from her shoulders on two narrow straps and ended at the highest possible point on her thighs.

As my wounds were still healing and I was in no condition to dance, I was glad that the $250 ticket to the party gave me access to a well-stocked bar that included Veuve Clicquot champagne. We partook of it steadily from our arrival at nine. It was while waiting for refills at the bar that I saw him, Chuck that is. He was sequestered away in a dark corner. A cloud of smoke created by a monstrous cigar swirled around him. Our eyes met, and he tipped his cigar in my direction. I abandoned my quest for champagne and walked over to his table.

"Have a seat," he said, pointing to the other chair.

I did. His sunburn was peeling.

"We need to talk about Aris," I said.

"About how she tried to—well, you're a smart boy. I'm sure you figured it out by now." Then he took a long draw.

"I want you to stay away from Aris."

"Now be nice. We'd both be a lot healthier if we stayed away from Aris, but Aris has an addictive quality, like smoking," he said, tapping his cigar against the ashtray. "And besides, I can do whatever I want. Remember, your future depends on me."

"Unless, of course, you killed Miles."

Chuck rolled his eyes. "Now, now. Let's not be slanderous."

"Now, now," I mocked. "We've got a motive—a guaranteed Supreme Court clerkship."

"No one would believe that. I was too successful as it was."

"Look, this may sound sentimental, but I love Aris. I want to marry her someday."

"Even after what happened in Lanai?"

"Go on," I said.

"What makes you think that Aris didn't lead you into that current?" He took another draw.

"Why would she?"

"The circumstantial evidence is strong. I had, after all, never been there. She'd snorkeled that very beach. 'There,'" said Chuck, affecting a high-pitched voice and pointing the way Aris had done, "'first one to find the turtle gets to spend the night with me.'"

"Perhaps she was hoping that you'd get caught in the current?" I rammed my index finger into his chest.

Chuck coughed and then tapped his ashes onto my hand. I jerked away.

"Perhaps."

"Why would Aris wish me any harm?" I asked.

"What if she killed Miles, and she thinks you're on to her. Miles was on the verge of wrecking her chances for a Supreme Court clerkship, too. You see, it all sounds stupid. No jury would buy it." He laughed.

"She spent the entire night with me. Besides, she must know that I love her and that even if… ."

"Even if what?" asked Chuck.

I was silent.

"Yes, I know. Even if you knew, you wouldn't tell."

I was still silent.

"Just remember," he said, "no person is above hurting another, even someone they love, if it's in their interest to do so."

"I don't believe that she intended to harm me. That's that."

"I've had enough sparring," said Chuck, yawning. "Meet me at my place, tomorrow at noon. Then if you still love Aris, she's all yours."

Chuck stood up and put his hand on my shoulder. "The year is growing short," he said.

I looked down at my watch. It was 11:52.

When I looked back up, Chuck was gone. I had not even felt him lift his hand from my shoulder.

I returned to the bar, devoid of any joyous champagne buzz, and managed to talk the bartender into parting with an entire bottle. I found Aris waiting impatiently at our table. She wondered what had taken me so long, but I just winked and led her to the dark corner table where Chuck and I had been sitting. I took Chuck's old chair and Aris climbed onto my lap, placing her wet mouth against my ear.

"I want you inside of me, now," she whispered, straddling me.

As the strange faces surrounding us counted down the last seconds of 1992, we made love silently in the shadows. Torn between my private rapture and what Chuck would reveal in 1993, I felt no sense of permanence or belonging. I had become another one of Chuck's pawns.

* * *

The next day I slept late. After bringing Aris some breakfast from the McDonald's downstairs, I said I had to get some beer for the day's bowl games. Instead, I headed toward Chuck's.

I was terribly anxious, like I used to feel waiting for the results at high school debate tournaments or going to pick up my grades in college, only worse. I loved Aris, and I honestly believed as I drove that nothing could change my mind. I tried to think of worst-case scenarios. What would I do if Aris had somehow participated in Miles's murder?

By the time that I arrived at Chuck's, my heart was pounding so hard that I could feel it in my eyes and hear it in my ears. When I knocked on his door, my palms were damp.

"Why, hello," Chuck said, opening the door. "Come on in. What I wanted to show you is on the coffee table."

As I got closer, I could see three porn magazines, each open to a nude picture of Aris, who was exposing herself.

"As you can see," said Chuck, "Aris has supplemented her income with a bit of amateur modeling." He picked one up.

"Indeed, this particular magazine was so thrilled with my Polaroid that they called nonstop for two weeks. They would've paid her $20,000 to do a centerfold."

I read the text printed below each of the pictures—Mary Tipton, Mona Jeffries, Lisa Stone. Pseudonyms. I gathered the two magazines from the table and snatched the third from Chuck's hands. I tried to walk to the door, but Chuck stepped in front of me, blocking my way.

"Do you still love her now?"

"I do, and a deal is a deal. Stay away from her." I pushed him aside.

"A deal is a deal, but remember ... reality is often inexplicable."

All I remember of the drive back is a feeling of relief.

When I returned to my apartment, Aris was in bed reading.

I tossed the rolled magazines onto the bed. "Chuck gave these to me."

Aris fainted.

It took me at least a minute to bring her to, at which point I said, "Do you hear me? I don't care."

She hugged me, clinging hard.

"Chuck sent them in," she said.

"I don't care."

"I was stupid and drunk. Chuck took out his Polaroid. We'd been having sex all evening, and I was feeling uninhibited. He promised not to show them to anyone. The next morning I woke up regretting it and made him give me the pictures back. Only he withheld a few. One day, he showed up, gloating, with one of those magazines and a check for $100. I called the magazine to complain. They had a copy of my driver's license. They had my signature on the release."

"Why didn't you press charges?"

"That was my first thought. But it would've merely drawn attention to the pictures. They would've been with me forever, part of the public record. Moreover, Chuck would've denied it. His forgery looked exactly like the signature on my driver's license."

"So you just decided to ignore them?" I asked.

"They're printed under false names. I bought every back copy from the publishers and burned them. I have no reason to believe that anyone recognized me."

"He'll always hold this over you."

"I promise you that he'll never make the pictures public."

"He's bound to have more copies in a safety deposit box someplace."

"I have something on him, too."

"Whatever it is, it didn't stop him from showing them to me. Why wouldn't he give them to others?"

"Just trust me."

I did. And Chuck, by all appearances, ceased his pursuit of Aris.

TWENTY-FOUR

Classes resumed. The Chicago winter went on, albeit warmer than I had anticipated because of Aris's nightly presence in my bed.

In mid-January, Chuck interviewed for a Supreme Court clerkship. A week later, the anticipated offer came by telephone, and Chuck accepted for the 1994-95 term, immediately following his Court of Appeals clerkship on the District of Columbia Circuit. During our occasional meetings, usually in the foyer or the Green Lounge, Chuck seemed a much happier, more relaxed person.

I too experienced blissful news in January, scoring an A+ on my elements of the law examination, the highest grade in the class, as well as an A- on my civil procedure exam. It appeared that I was well on my way to the *Law Review*.

Aris's chance at the Supremes didn't come until February 15. She received an offer at the conclusion of her interview and accepted it on the spot. Like Chuck, she agreed to serve during the 1994-95 term, immediately following her Court of Appeals clerkship on the Fourth Circuit in Virginia. When Aris returned from Washington, she was the happiest I had ever seen her. She had, after all, won the big game.

Even Lee had regained his old swagger. By virtue of his getting onto *Law Review* in a timely manner, he was hired by Chuck's judge on the D.C. Circuit. According to Chuck, this was due in large part to his recommendation.

All in all, it seemed that everything was back to normal. People had pretty much forgotten about Miles. People didn't even see the tattered signs offering the reward anymore. That was, until an extraordinarily warm day in early March, when temperatures rose into the sixties and melted the snow pack all the way down to gray mud.

A maintenance worker saw something in the field behind the law school's parking lot: a Gucci wallet, Miles Vanderlyden's stolen Gucci wallet.

I knew something was up when I pulled into the parking lot and found the adjacent field surrounded by yellow crime scene tape. A dozen suited men were peering into the muck.

Two days later, there was a message from Agent Zero: "We would like to ask you a few questions. I'll see you at the Federal Building on Jackson, room 418, tomorrow morning at nine."

Aris seemed terrified by the whole business and couldn't sleep the night before my questioning. I didn't fare much better. Despite my exhaustion, I walked down to the FBI offices, where I was eventually led to a white room with no windows, a card table, and three chairs. I took a seat and waited a couple of minutes before the all-too-familiar Zero arrived, along with a district attorney.

They both shook my hand and sat down.

"I should start by telling you the current state of our investigation," said Zero. "The reward turned up absolutely nothing. Sure, crack heads called like nuts, but not one legitimate lead. Then there was that troubling fact of the Coke bottle, and now Mr. Vanderlyden's wallet appears. Not one credit card missing. While there was no cash in the wallet's main compartment, there was more than a hundred dollars in small bills behind the credit cards. According to his family, that's where Mr. Vanderlyden always put excess cash. While crack heads aren't necessarily fond of credit cards, they do tear wallets to pieces looking for hidden cash."

"Perhaps the killer dropped the wallet while he was fleeing from the police."

"True, but that wouldn't explain why this poor crack head was wearing cashmere and wool."

"Excuse me?"

"When we examined the body, the murder weapon, and other evidence from the office, we found so many different fibers that we couldn't determine which fibers belonged to the murderer. But in the main pocket of the wallet, where one would usually carry cash, we found two unusual fibers that matched others present on Mr. Vanderlyden and the book. The fibers, however, don't match what Mr. Vanderlyden was wearing the day he was killed—or any other clothing belonging to him. These are some pretty fine examples of wool and cashmere. Neither fabric is typically worn by your average drug addict."

"What does that have to do with me?"

"Do you remember what Mr. Gibbs was wearing the night of Mr. Vanderlyden's death?"

"It's been so long. I have no idea."

"Have you ever seen Mr. Gibbs wear anything with a wool lining or cuff?"

"I'm not sure I even know what wool looks like."

"This is a particular kind of wool—a raw, cream-colored wool that's used on cuffs and lapels of jackets, sometimes as the lining of coats or gloves."

"I know what you're talking about."

"What kind of coat does Gibbs usually wear?" asked Zero.

"Long, dark brown overcoat."

"Does it have cream-colored cuffs?"

"I'm pretty sure it doesn't."

"What about his gloves?"

"I don't know."

"That will be all." Zero got up and left with his companion.

I went back home. As soon as I opened the door, Aris was upon me. "Lee's been calling all morning."

I picked up the phone and dialed.

"Hello?" I recognized Lee's voice.

"This is Gray."

"They're here right now with a search warrant. They're taking all my clothes."

"They're looking for wool and cashmere fibers," I said.

"I know. That's what the search warrant said."

"Is there anything I can do?"

"Gray … I think I'm about to be arrested."

"I know you didn't do it."

"I've got to go."

"Bye."

Aris and I didn't go to class that day. When we turned on

the WGN news at noon, Lee was the lead story: "From Cook County Jail comes late word that there has finally been a break in the murder of University of Chicago law student Miles Vanderlyden. Kathy," said the anchorman.

"Yes," said a female reporter standing on some steps, "Chicago Police, with the help of the FBI's crime lab, may have finally solved the December murder of law student Miles Vanderlyden. Just minutes ago, Lee Gibbs, another student, was arrested and brought here for booking. The break came when the victim's wallet was found in the melting snow behind the law school, where it had apparently been frozen since December. According to the FBI, fibers found on the wallet provided the break that led to Mr. Gibbs's arrest."

The anchorman returned. "As soon as we learn more about the Vanderlyden murder, we'll let you know. Now, on to other news... ."

TWENTY-FIVE

Over the next few weeks, Lee's saga went on in the background of our lives. Lee said that the FBI had not yet found a match on the cashmere fibers from the crime scene. But the wool fibers from the lining of his gloves were an exact match. According to Lee's attorney, however, thousands of wool-lined gloves and jackets used the same fiber.

Nonetheless, the evidence regarding the wool fibers, the fingerprints on the Coke bottle, Lee's motive of getting on the *Law Review*, and his admitting to spending the night alone in the library were plenty to get Lee indicted for murder. The judge denied him bail, regarding his family wealth as a flight risk.

When I visited Lee at the Cook County Jail, usually once a week, he often showed signs of being physically beaten, but he refused to provide any details. All he could do was talk about his hope that the Illinois Court of Appeals would reverse the judge's decision on bail. Unfortunately, the panel of judges summarily denied Lee's petition.

I felt sorry for Lee and sorry for myself, sorry I didn't have the courage to go to the police with what I knew about Chuck. If someone at the law school had killed Miles, it was Chuck. Chuck possessed a virulent jealousy for Miles. He desperately wanted to be editor-in-chief. He was furious with Miles for getting what Chuck regarded as "his" job. Chuck's Supreme Court clerkship was in jeopardy because of the Kupow business. Miles had threatened to turn Chuck's blackmail against him. Chuck knew that Miles would be working really late. Chuck lived close enough that he had the opportunity to walk to the law school. Certainly the police needed to know all this. And then, in a flash, I remembered that Chuck had worn a wool-cuffed coat on the night of Miles's murder and that Chuck had once advised me to buy cashmere-lined gloves. I tried to remember whether I had ever seen him wear either that coat or those gloves after the night of the murder. I didn't think that he had.

I called Aris at the *Law Review* office.

"I'm going to tell the police what I know about Chuck."

"You can't do that."

"They've got to know."

"I can't talk here. Do you know where Ida Noyes Hall is, across the Midway?" she asked.

"Yes."

"I'm going there for dinner with some *Law Review* people. Meet me on the rooftop terrace at ten."

"Sure."

"Just promise me you won't do anything until we talk."

"I promise."

I spent the afternoon thinking about Lee. Even though he had been an absentee friend these last few months, he had gone out of his way to help me in college. We had become instant friends after sitting together at a dinner where his fraternity was evaluating prospective new members. Lee's enthusiastic support for my membership overcame the opposition of others in the fraternity who thought I wasn't up to its usual standards. Now, Lee desperately needed my support, and I felt like I was betraying him by keeping silent about Chuck.

So I headed down Lake Shore Drive, resolved to stand firm regardless of what Aris had to say. I would go to Agent Zero in the morning and do the right thing.

I pulled into a parking space on the Midway, went into Ida Noyes Hall, and took the stairs up to a rooftop ballroom. I walked across the creaky wood floor and pushed open a door leading to the deserted terrace. It was a nice night for the end of March, low fifties, clear, no wind. I leaned against the railing and admired the view over the spires and gargoyles of the gothic campus.

Aris walked up beside me. "What were you thinking mentioning Chuck on the phone?"

"I'm sorry."

"Either the *Law Review* phone or your phone could be tapped."

"I'm convinced he did it."

"We've talked about your theories before. What's different now? Do you really believe that Chuck would kill Miles for a Supreme Court clerkship?"

"Perhaps Chuck didn't intend to kill him. Maybe he was just repeating his blackmail threat, only there was a fight. Remember, Chuck was wearing a wool-cuffed coat and cashmere gloves. Have you seen Chuck wear that coat or those gloves since then?"

"You can't go to the police about Chuck," she begged. "Think about those pictures. He'd ruin me too."

"You're willing to let Lee rot in jail rather than suffer a little embarrassment?"

"No, no, no," I heard Chuck say from behind us.

We turned.

"Trust me," he said, "those pictures are the least of her worries, and yours. If what you tell the police implicates me in Miles's murder, I'll take Aris with me, as a coconspirator."

Aris started to cry. "Please, please. Gray. Don't you love me?"

"Of course Gray loves you," said Chuck. "But the question before Gray is whether he loves you more than Lee Gibbs. Or perhaps I'm overstating Mr. Bullock's altruism. Perhaps Mr. Bullock would better understand the situation if I framed it in terms of what will happen to him—besides having his beloved go to prison."

I stepped toward Chuck. I seriously considered throwing him over the balcony.

"Wait, wait. Hear me out," said Chuck, pulling a small semiautomatic pistol from his sport coat.

I backed away.

"One," he said, "your testimony gets you obstruction of justice, no matter what happens to me. You covered up information that was obviously relevant, and you misled the FBI. You may not go to jail, but you can kiss your little legal career goodbye. Two ... if they nail me, I'll do my best to take you down. Remember, you did drive me home. Three ... you might never make it home tonight. Hyde Park is, after all, a very rough neighborhood.

People get shot for no apparent reason," said Chuck, cocking the pistol and aiming it directly at my face.

"Gray, please listen to him." Aris was in tears as the bells of the adjacent chapel began to bong the hour.

When they stopped, Chuck lowered the gun. "The evidence against your friend Lee is meager. Even if his case goes to trial, he probably won't be found guilty. You have nothing to lose by waiting to see what happens."

"True," I said, moving closer to Chuck, still thinking about how I could overpower him.

He lifted the gun again, and I raised my hands. "As for you," he said, "things are going well. It looks like you're well on your way to grading onto *Law Review*. Remember, I control the appointment of the next editor-in-chief, and he'll owe me. Come next spring, the new chief will have enormous sway over his own replacement. I can arrange it so that his replacement is you. I can also ensure that you'll be hired by an impressive Court of Appeals judge, probably mine. In December 1994, Aris and I will be sifting clerkship applications at the Supreme Court. We can get you interviews."

I turned around, leaned against the terrace railing, and stared at the chapel next door. "You're right, I don't have anything to lose by waiting to see whether Lee is acquitted."

I had surrendered.

Aris put her arm around me. "He's left," she said.

"I know." I was shivering with fear.

TWENTY-SIX

The months went on, and my visits to Lee at the jail became less frequent as I returned to the minutiae of my own life. I did everything I could to convince Chuck that I was on board. Yet whenever I walked in the darkness, I awaited the report of Chuck's gun. Night after night, my sleep was broken by the burning heat of the bullet that I thought was sure to come.

I took refuge from my terror in my studies, and it showed in the results. My grades from winter quarter were excellent, an A- in contracts and an A in torts. I finished my spring quarter exams in early June, feeling just as good about my performance on those exams. Chuck even helped me get a job as a summer research assistant for Professor Rittinger. Meanwhile, he and Aris both graduated with high honors and moved off to D.C. and Virginia, respectively, to start their clerkships. I flew out to visit Aris every weekend that summer. Despite the distance, we were spending more time together than ever.

In July, we were all relieved when the business with Lee finally resolved itself short of trial, just as Chuck had predicted. After the FBI was unable to find a match on the mystery cashmere fiber and never found any blood, hair, or other fibers from Miles on any of Lee's clothing, the judge accepted Lee's motion to dismiss the case for lack of evidence. Lee planned to return to school that fall, but he had spent two quarters of school in jail. In order to graduate, each student must take nine quarters of classes. Lee was two quarters behind and could not graduate until March 1995, well beyond the June 1994 starting time for his D.C. Circuit clerkship. While it would have been hard to imagine the court allowing Lee to clerk given all that had transpired, it was a convenient excuse for the judge to hire someone else and for Lee to get on with his life. Strangely enough, it didn't seem to bother him. He was just happy to be free.

On August 1, my last exam grades came in, all A's with the exception of one B. While I wasn't number one in my class, I wasn't too far behind. A week later, my appraisal of my class standing was confirmed by an official package from the *Review*, welcoming me into its membership. I had, after all, hand-delivered my application. That was one other lesson that I had learned from Lee.

My personal life with Aris continued to improve over the summer. On Labor Day weekend, I took Aris to visit my parents. By all appearances, they adored her. Basking in my parents' approval and the familiarity of home, I decided to ask her to marry me. On Saturday, when Aris and my mom were visiting the Houston Museum of Fine Arts, I revealed my intentions to my father. He was so thrilled that he took me down to the Galleria and cosigned my credit application so that I could purchase a spectacular 2.5 carat engagement ring. It would take me seven years to pay for it, but I wanted everyone to know how special she was to me.

That night, I borrowed my dad's station wagon and took Aris to Transco Park. The centerpiece of the park is a giant man-made, half-circle waterfall that towers three stories. Amid its blowing mist, I got down on one knee and proposed. She accepted with a long, slow kiss.

Aris set our wedding for Saturday, June 17, 1995 at her father's country estate, just west of Charlottesville. Over the next two years, we spent many a weekend driving between his estate and Aris's apartment in northern Virginia. He was charming, and we became good friends.

As a result of my frequent trips to Virginia, I also became acquainted with Aris's employer, whom everyone referred to affectionately as "The Judge." He is an avid jogger, and Aris and I frequently joined him for his Saturday morning run along the Mall in D.C. By February of 1994, he had offered me a clerkship for the 1995-96 term. I proudly accepted.

Of all things, we also started attending church services. Neither of us had grown up in particularly religious families. We went to church at Easter and Christmas. That was about it. But Aris's coclerk was a member of a small Lutheran church in Falls Church. He coaxed us into attending services that first Easter in 1994. We ended up going back again and again, eventually becoming members of the congregation just before Christmas, while Aris was clerking for the Supreme Court.

Aris's newfound spirituality was so fervent that she declared sex off-limits until our wedding night. At first I found her request strange. But the more I thought about it, the more it made sense given her once ambiguous sexual ethics.

But the real reason for her religious zeal did not reveal itself until a few weeks later, in early February of 1995. It was one of the few weekends that Aris traveled to Chicago instead of me to Virginia. Her uncle, who lived in Michigan, was on vacation, and he offered us his country house, a rustic cabin on tree-lined Eagle Lake, for the weekend. Between two and three feet of snow lay on the ground when we arrived. Eagle Lake was frozen solid, the white ice gleaming beneath a full moon. Despite our being exhausted from the drive, Aris insisted that we go snowmobiling in the moonlight. We borrowed snowmobile suits and helmets from her uncle's wardrobe closet and fired up the machines. They were easy enough to drive in the snow, but terribly tricky on the frozen lake. One sharp turn, and donut spinning was the immediate result. This was unsettling at first, but the deep snow banks that lined the lake always stopped us without risk of injury.

About an hour into our play, Aris stopped her snowmobile in the middle of the lake and turned off its engine. I pulled up beside her and did the same.

"That night at the Snow Ball," she began, speaking barely above a whisper, "Chuck kept complaining about how Miles had destroyed our chances at Supreme Court clerkships. I jokingly suggested that Chuck ought to have Miles killed, because then everyone would suspect Cardenas. Chuck got this evil glimmer in his eye and said: 'And you're going to help me do it.'

"Chuck rambled on about how it would be better to make it look like a botched robbery, like the robber had just meant to knock him out. Chuck thought that would bring less scrutiny from the FBI. 'Ordinary crime,' he said.

"But then he decided that the FBI scrutiny would already be there because of Cardenas. The thing to do, he said, would be to suggest ordinary crime, but to make it look like a cover up for someone else. That someone else was Lee. I had already told him about Lee's twisted fantasy, and we both had noticed Lee sleeping in the library at night. It was a nested setup. The FBI would look for a professional hit and find a robbery. Maybe it would still end as a botched robbery. If not, nested behind the robbery would be evidence pointing toward Lee. The motive would be solidified because Chuck would immediately admit him to the *Review*. The opportunity would be there because Lee would have spent the night in the library frantically working on the article revisions we had assigned to him. The method of killing Miles would be very close to Lee's fantasy, which you would confirm when questioned. Finally, Chuck cemented the frame-up by taking Lee's empty Coke bottle from the library carrel where Lee studied, which would link him to the scene of the crime. As for us, Chuck's theory was that precisely because of our great success, we wouldn't be suspected. He was right."

"But why?" I asked.

"I saw Miles's murder as the only way to free myself from Chuck."

"Those silly pictures?"

"There was more."

"I want to know."

"He made me do unconscionable things." She looked down at the ice but was strangely expressionless.

"Tell me," I urged.

She raised her blank eyes to me and then looked back at the ice. "He once took me to the Hotel Nikko bar for karaoke. You know, where all the Asian businessmen drink the night away. I remember my first champagne cocktail tasting funny. Then everything started to spin. My memory of the night is limited to snapshots of an instant here, another there. In the hotel elevator. On my back in a bed. Different men on top of me. Chuck taking money from them. I woke up the next morning at my apartment, in my own bed. But I was really sore and had a terrible headache. I knew what had happened. Even if I could've proven it, I was too embarrassed, too concerned about what my dad would think, about my career."

The image made me ill, and I silently swore that one day I would make Chuck pay for what he had done to us.

"You see," she said, "if I could get Chuck to kill Miles, I would own Chuck. On the other hand, if something went wrong, I knew that Chuck would quickly kill himself to avoid prison. I'd be free of him either way, and there would be no one to implicate me. Indeed, the night of the murder, Chuck had cyanide with him."

"Why would Chuck, with all he has going for him—"

"While Chuck sometimes claimed a working class background, his childhood was really much worse. He grew up in the slums south of the law school, in destitute poverty, beaten daily by the gangs and by his own single mother, who spent most of her time turning tricks to buy drugs. His father was just another john from the north side, some rich college kid who paid double not to have to wear a condom. Chuck hasn't seen his mother since he was sixteen, when he applied for and received a scholarship to boarding school. You can understand why Chuck hated us all so much. Things only got worse after Miles used his family power to squeeze Chuck out of his hard-won position as editor-in-chief. That was the night he took me to the Nikko."

I tried to stop my welling tears as she coolly continued.

"Even before that, though, Chuck was never interested in some upper-middle-class life of comfort. He wanted all or nothing. He was perfectly willing to give up the hold he had over me in exchange for editor-in-chief, a Supreme Court clerkship, and all the power that followed. Chuck wants to be President of the United States. He believed that Miles's death could transform him into a sympathetic figure, put to rest all of the controversy over Mary Kupow, and propel him toward his ultimate goal. He was right.

"Yet he had an alternative plan, short of murder, that he had devised all by himself. He had run into Susan, Miles's ex-girlfriend, on Michigan Avenue. We both knew Miles still had feelings for Susan despite his engagement to Katie. Chuck convinced Susan that Katie was a poor match for Miles, that it was an arranged marriage of some kind. That's why Susan conspired with Chuck to try to end their engagement at the Snow Ball.

"Things went so perfectly that night. You should have heard the things that Miles said in his moment of passion, which Chuck conveniently recorded on a hidden camera. We couldn't have scripted it any better. I was so afraid that Miles would do anything to keep his embarrassing mess a secret. But he rejected the threat of revelation and returned the threat. That response necessitated the murder.

"Chuck went behind Miles with the big book. When Miles finished talking, Chuck smacked him as hard as he could in the back of the head. Only Chuck doesn't eat much, and he wasn't strong enough to do the job. Sure, Miles fell down. He'd been knocked a bit silly, but the first blow just gave him a minor concussion, if that. Chuck had to kneel over Miles and pound him with the book again and again until his skull finally cracked open. The cracking sound was so loud that I was sure someone had heard. As much as it was what I wanted, it was horrible, so horrible. On that last blow, blood splattered up on Chuck's gloves, so he had to go to the bathroom to try to wash it off. The cashmere fibers, of course, came from the lining on Chuck's gloves, which he wore to avoid leaving his own prints on the Coke bottle and the book.

"Then you showed up. We had to keep you out of the office and away for a few minutes so that we could be sure that Miles was dead. While you were down below waiting, we watched as Miles took his last breaths. Then we cleaned out the petty cash and took Miles's wallet and watch.

"When Chuck went to his car in the parking lot, he checked the wallet for cash and tossed it into the snow, expecting the police to find it there the next morning. I took Miles's watch with me. After you fell asleep, I dropped it down the trash shoot into your building's incinerator. Meanwhile, Chuck didn't go directly back to his apartment. He waited for us to leave and then walked around the corner and gave his coat to a homeless man who was warming himself in front of a trash can. While the guy was trying on the coat, Chuck dropped his gloves into the fire. Finally, when we were questioned the next morning, we each revealed different parts of the Lee puzzle, to get the FBI pointing in his direction. The only loose end was—"

"Me."

With that, Aris restarted her snowmobile and headed back to the house. I was alone on the ice.

* * *

Aris has never mentioned that night again. I have long forgiven her of everything, including what happened in Hawaii. And me, well, earlier today I graduated with high honors from the most competitive law school in the country after serving as the editor-in-chief of the *Law Review*. This Saturday, I'm moving to Virginia, where I'm going to marry the only woman I've ever loved. I'll spend the next year under the tutelage of one of the most respected judges on the Court of Appeals. The year after that I'll be clerking at the Supreme Court. I'm well on my way to realizing my dream of serving in the Senate.

My parents say I lead a charmed life—well almost. From time to time something reminds me of Miles. I'm unsure even today why I never went to the police. Love, sex, power, money, fear, or even just inertia. But I didn't participate in Miles's murder, and nothing could have brought him back. Chuck and Aris are in God's hands now. Aris knows that too. Every day at lunch she finds an open church, any church, and prays in silence amid the empty pews.

As for Lee, I suppose there's a chance that my testimony could have saved him four months of jail, but I didn't put him there in the first instance. Professor Rittinger once explained the Good Samaritan Rule in his torts class. If you put someone in a dangerous position, you're obligated to help him out of it. If not, you possess no duty to render aid, even if the aid costs you little. Helping Lee, however, would have cost me a lot. I would have sacrificed everything—Aris, the *Law Review*, the clerkships, my entire legal career, perhaps even my life. I wonder, though, what I would have done had Lee been convicted. Would my conscience have finally overwhelmed my desire?

Whatever the case, I never had to make that decision. Decision. I think decision itself is a misnomer. It implies that a choice existed for me at the final moment. More often than not, though, one becomes embroiled in adversity not from a single bad decision, but rather from a series of little decisions that were fine when they were made. By the time I knew where my decisions had led me, all of my options save one were effectively foreclosed—by my love for Aris, by my sense of self-preservation.

But I still think about Miles's last moments. I see him falling, confused. I wonder what it must have been like for Aris, what it's like for Aris now, beneath her veil of composure. And Chuck, did he feel the panic and horror of an irreversible wrong? Or did he smile triumphantly? No, whenever I'm tempted to pass judgment, I remember. I remember what transpired between us that dark winter. At one time or another, we all dance with obsession.

S. Scott Gaille was a member of the Law Review at the University of Chicago Law School. He graduated with high honors in 1995 and then clerked for the United States Court of Appeals for the Fourth Circuit. He now practices law and writes in Houston.